RED RUNS THE RIVER

for the library of my
Alma Mater
Nyack College

Anthony Bollback
Class of '43
Alumnus of the Year 2000

RED RUNS THE RIVER

The Story of China's Persecuted Church, Vol.1

ANTHONY G. BOLLBACK

Pleasant Word

Packaged by Pleasant Word, PO Box 428, Enumclaw, WA 98022. The views expressed or implied in this work do not necessarily reflect those of Pleasant Word. The author(s) is ultimately responsible for the design, content and editorial accuracy of this work.

Unless otherwise noted, all Scriptures are taken from the Holy Bible, New International Version, Copyright © 1973, 1978, 1984 by the International Bible Society. Used by permission of Zondervan Publishing House. The "NIV" and "New International Version" trademarks are registered in the United States Patent and Trademark Office by International Bible Society.

Scripture references marked KJV are taken from the King James Version of the Bible.

Scripture references marked NASB are taken from the New American Stan-dard Bible, © 1960, 1963, 1968, 1971, 1972, 1973, 1975, 1977 by The Lockman Foundation. Used by permission.

ISBN 1-4141-0110-4
Library of Congress Catalog Card Number: 2003116905

DEDICATION

*In loving memory of the thousands of Chinese Christians
who chose to follow Jesus Christ in death
rather than renounce their faith in Him;
of such this world was not worthy.*

TABLE OF CONTENTS

FOREWORD

Communism destroys. That was my conclusion after twenty years of missionary service in Vietnam. And Communism has a particular vendetta against the church of Jesus Christ. Through lies, threats, privation, torture, imprisonment, and persecution it hopes to stamp out the church. But Communism is a slow-learner. The more it persecutes the church, the more the church multiplies! Anthony Bollback has witnessed first-hand this amazing, glorious phenomenon. He illustrates it masterfully in *Red Runs the River.*

The first few pages, setting up the story, are spellbinders. You will have a difficult time putting the book down. As you read on you will begin to feel a little of what it is like to live and die for a faith that lasts forever.

Bollback draws the central characters in part from his memories of missionary life in China. You'll find him a skilled storyteller. But Anthony has another reason for using the fiction genre in this book. He needs to protect the identities of places where *right now* some of these exploits for God are happening and the humble servants of God who, by God's Spirit, are making them happen.

Here is an instructive, moving story of church growth in China despite the unbelievable obstacles. But the book is more. From beginning to end, it is packed with rewarding insights as to how believers—even American believers—can trust in God.

Red Runs the River is predicated on experience, passion, and principle. The author has had a fruitful missionary career in China, Hong Kong, and Japan. In addition, he has been an effective church-planter and pastor, a compassionate, respected church leader and the author of several other missionary books.

Red Runs the River is more than just a first-class love story. It is a wake-up call you can respond to. It combines truth, hope, and love in a drama built around authentic human situations. This story will challenge you to pray with greater understanding for your Christian brothers and sisters in China. You will gain a deeper appreciation for the amazing triumphs that Christ's persecuted Church is experiencing there.

It is a book calculated to build your faith. Even as it drives you to pray for the persecuted church in China—and in many other nations—its reports of church growth will encourage you.

Dr. Thomas H. Stebbins, Former Executive Director International Evangelism Explosion Fort Lauderdale, Florida

INTRODUCTION

The martyrdom of John and Betty Stam, missionaries of the China Inland Mission, in December 1934, made an indelible impression on me as a young boy. Their heroic sacrifice and martyrdom had a definite part in my commitment to missionary service in China, and although unknown to me at the time, the eventual impetus for this book. *Red Runs the River* is the heroic story of thousands of Chinese Christians who sealed their testimony with their own blood. Several hundred years ago when the gospel first came to the Middle Kingdom, now known as China, the river of blood started flowing. It became a raging torrent when the Communist regime took power in 1949 under the harsh repression of Mao Zedong. It is estimated that 30 million Chinese died under the cruel heel of Mao and his regime. Today, thousands of Christians still languish in China's prisons for no other reason than their faith in Jesus Christ.

I will never forget the anguish we suffered as missionaries of The Christian and Missionary Alliance when we were forced to evacuate China at the time of the Communist takeover in 1949. We became painfully aware of the high cost of discipleship when we heard about many of our Chinese colleagues who were imprisoned for long years of re-indoctrination. At that time we could only imagine the suffering they were enduring. One such man, Rev. Joshua Ku, our dear friend and colleague, was the pastor of the growing Christian and Missionary Alliance Church in Wuchang. He was imprisoned for twenty years, and yet stalwartly refused to renounce his faith in Jesus Christ. Upon release from prison, he immediately gathered a group of young people together for the purpose of training them for ministry.

Returning to work with the Chinese people in Hong Kong from 1957 to 1970, I had opportunity to hear firsthand reports of the thousands of believers who had laid down their lives for Christ. My wife and I lived through the invasion of refugees into Hong Kong during the mid 1960s at the height of the Red Guard rampage in China. We witnessed the tragic roundup of these destitute people who were sent back to China and probably death. The cries of people in boarded up trains, begging for the chance of freedom, are cries that ring in our memories to this very day.

Although I have carried the seeds of this story for many years, it was not until 2002 that the Lord pressed upon me the urgent need to write about the river of blood. In many mission conferences over the years in hundreds of churches, I have used as my text the words of Jesus found in Matthew 16:18, "On this rock I will build my church, and the gates of hell shall not prevail against it." There is no doubt that in spite of the hundreds and hundreds of accounts of believers suffering and forgotten in horrible prisons and forced labor camps at the hands of cruel men who were determined to wipe out the testimony of Jesus Christ, the church in China has grown at a phenomenal rate. Although I chose to write this fascinating story of victory and challenge as historical fiction, the characters are composites of people known to me who endured unspeakable suffering. There is documentation to verify many of the accounts of the heartless persecution of stalwart believers who dared to live and die for Christ with victory and praise on their lips.

As I prayed about writing this story, God led me to weave the authentic reports of persecution into a fictional story of two young people who suffered the intense sting of persecution and many years of forced separation. In spite of their terrible hardships, they never wavered in their faith and devotion to Jesus Christ, just as hundreds of Chinese, past and present.

Because of the underlying truth of each fictional episode, *Red Runs the River* is much more than fiction. It is the story of heroic followers of Jesus Christ who paid the ultimate price for their love and devotion to Him. The result is that a very unusual phenomenon is occurring in China. Throughout the land of China where the Communists vowed to stamp out Christianity, the greatest movement of God in the history of the nation is taking place. Although China has done its worst to wipe out every vestige of Christianity, every tactic has failed. Today there is an estimated 80 to 100 million Christians in China, whereas at the time of the Communist takeover, there were only an estimated one or two million believers in the whole country! God's church is flourishing.

My prayer is that every reader will be impacted by the gripping stories of the faithfulness and courage of the Chinese Christians in their hour of trial. We in America have not been tested as our Chinese brothers and sisters. Too often we are caught up by materialism and compromise. We are spiritually asleep. May this story be a wake-up call to prepare Christians to face the inevitable persecution of the end times. And may the response be to follow Jesus at whatever cost as the brave Christians in China have done so well and so faithfully.

I owe a great debt to my wife Evelyn of sixty years for her dedicated commitment to serving the Lord by my side, and for her invaluable help and suggestions for this story. Without her sage advice and encouragement, this story would never have seen the light of day. I am also deeply indebted to my daughter, Joy Peters, who has edited all of my previous books, and who tackled this one with skill and commitment to Jesus. *Red Runs the River* is the culmination of my life-long passion to serve the Chinese people and Christ's church; I send it forth with the hope that it will bring many people face to face with Jesus.

Anthony G. Bollback
Kissimmee, Florida,
2004

WHAT OTHERS ARE SAYING ABOUT

Red Runs The River

Since the Communist takeover, every "China Hand" (missionaries who served in China) has lived with two kinds of pain. The first, leaving a part of themselves behind when we had to depart that beloved land, and second, the agony of soul in knowing of the persecuted church that must remain. Anthony Bollback, with sensitive insight and skill, has shown us another side: the story of how that church has survived in triumph. China Hand or not, the reader will be deeply moved with this account. Though by necessity fiction, it is exciting and historically accurate. Read it and weep—and laugh—and rejoice.

Dr. Edwin Kilbourne
Vice President at Large
OMS International, A China Hand

This is a book born of passion, passion that Anthony Bollback has for the Chinese people. His years in China gave him the rich background and real-life experiences to write a gripping story that wraps romance, adventure, danger, and triumph around the keen historical perspective of the times in which it was set. This is a wonderful work that will grab your attention and capture your heart.

Dr. David F. Presher
Vice President Advancement,
The Christian & Missionary Alliance

Anthony Bollback, an outstanding missionary to Asia and a denominational leader, has produced in this book *Red Runs the River,* a thrilling and yet sad story on the conquest of the church in China during the last half-century. In following the happenings that took place in China when the Communists took over, he has captured in novel form the sufferings of those in China who have paid such a costly price to follow the Lord. He weaves a beautiful love story into the accounts of their hardships. All age groups will gain much through reading these stories.

Dr. Paul L. Alford,
Former President
Toccoa Falls College

Seasoned author Anthony Bollback has been a Christian missionary to China and Hong Kong for many years, and he is in tune with the Chinese people, their past and present history. Readers of this book will feel the heartbeat of that great nation portrayed in real conditions and characters captured in an engrossing drama.

Dr. Wayne Frair,
former Chairman of the Biology Department,
Kings College, NY

In a day when the children of our nation are being inundated with material totally alien to the claims of Christ, it is refreshing and uplifting to read a story of hope and love based on the extensive mission field experience of the author, Anthony Bollback. His writing not only captures the imagination, it promotes a knowledge of God as real and present in people. It will build character. I recommend that you use this book with your children and make it available to young people in your sphere of influence. I intend to do so.

Dr. John Bechtel
Executive Director, The DeMoss Foundation

Life-changing in its challenges and adventurous in its presentation, *Red Runs the River* takes the reader in story form through breathtaking, unimaginable human experiences occurring in the Communist takeover and oppression of China. Anthony Bollback masterfully reveals genuine human aspirations, concerns, and longings in the lives of Meiling and Anching, Chinese young people. Their experiences reveal the hand of God in the midst of disappointments and even suffering. The secret of their courage is presented in striking reality. *Red Runs the River* will capture your every emotion with refreshing honesty while demonstrating the greatest fulfillment and satisfaction for any life in the 21st century.

Dr. Mark T. O'Farrell
Southeastern District Superintendent,
The Christian & Missionary Alliance

OTHER BOOKS BY THE AUTHOR

To China and Back—The Story of Anthony and Evelyn
Bollback
Giants Walked Among Us—The Story of Paul and Ina Bartel

Children's Books

The Jack and Jenny Mystery Series:
Smugglers in Hong Kong
Capture of the Twin Dragon
The Mystery of the Counterfeit Money
Rescue at Cripple Creek
The Tiger Shark Strikes Again
Japan—Land of Great Surprises

All book descriptions and how to obtain them are found on
the author's web site *www.bollback.com*
or by contacting him by e-mail at *Kahu@juno.com*

Chapter 1

SIGNS OF THE TIMES

The dark, ominous clouds of civil war drifted over Central China at the close of World War II as the Communist army of Mao Zedong relentlessly crept south. Fear clutched at the hearts of young and old alike as they anxiously watched the fierce struggle for the mind of the nation.

A sense of helplessness enveloped them, as it seemed one Chinese army was as bad as the other. The soldiers of Chiang Kaishek, commander of the Nationalist army, were often cruel and heartless, and frequently confiscated the last ounce of rice the people had. On the other hand, the Chinese Communist army promised conditions would be different once they gained control. Everyone's rice bowl would be full, and that sounded good to desperate people. Still, disturbing and persistent reports drifting south, carried on the lips of fleeing refugees, told a story of unbearable hardships and even death to those who opposed Mao's troops.

Puyang is a quiet little suburb of Wuchang, one of the three major cities in the great industrial triangle of Wuhan. It lies on the south side of the mighty Yangtze River while Hankou and Hangyang are on the north side. Life moved at a leisure pace in Puyang, as it had for centuries, and most people believed it would never change. Under the able supervision of Mr. Woo, a Columbia University graduate, his high school offered students the best education available in the region.

Sitting in his office, he thought, *If only the times were more peaceful and this ugly war was far away. Perhaps Puyang would remain peaceful and I would live long enough to see my children marry, and have many grandsons.* Suddenly, his thoughts were interrupted by raucous shouting in the street. Hurrying to the window, he looked out on a scene that sent shivers up his spine. A large group of angry students from the nearby university were parading past the school, banners waving, shouting anti-government slogans.

Several weeks passed without further incident, but then one day, as school was being dismissed, a crowd of noisy students suddenly appeared, rushing toward the school. Principal Woo's daughter, Meiling and her friends, were just leaving the school grounds when the crowd burst on the scene. Surprised by the suddenness of the demonstrators, she and her friends backed away, but not before she spied the brother of one of her friends in the group of shouting students.

"There's your brother," she said. "He's leading the group in a Mao chant."

Her friend looked shocked, and then slowly replied, "I didn't know he was involved in the student uprising." she said in surprise, "But he has been acting strange lately and he always is talking politics."

As the girls attempted to hide behind other students, the brother caught sight of them. Pointing his finger at them, he shouted, "There she is. Meiling, the daughter of the principal of this school who is a lackey of the government."

Everyone riveted their eyes on Meiling and her friends as they vainly tried to hide. It was as if a knife had sliced through the crowd as they quickly separated from the girls. There they stood, exposed and embarrassed, and trembling with apprehension. The brother harangued the crowd about the rich principal who was oppressing the masses and leading them astray with his old-fashioned philosophies of education and life.

The crowd surged toward the girls as they stood exposed and forsaken. Too late. There was nowhere to turn. The brother rushed toward his sister, shouting, "Go home and do your kitchen work. Leave this enemy of our state or I will punish you severely."

In the melee that followed, Meiling's books were knocked from her hands and scattered under the trampling feet of the college ruffians. Anching, a senior high school student from one of the poorest homes in the community, watched with dismay as the crowd roughed up Meiling who now wept openly as she stood, humiliated and afraid. For almost a year since he had been admitted to this private school on a scholarship, he had observed this beautiful girl with the flashing eyes and the swinging braids of shiny black hair. She was an outstanding athlete and captain of the volleyball team. Whenever opportunity arose, he lingered near the court to catch a glimpse of her as she played with so much enthusiasm and skill, always leading the team with magnificent plays that made them winners on most occasions. Although they were not in the same social class, he treasured every moment when he glimpsed her passing in the halls or on the playing field. No question about it. He was attracted to this lovely girl, but he moved in different circles. There was a great gulf between them. She was from the elite of the town, poised, and beautiful, but unaware that he even existed. He hated the poverty that relegated him to the lowest of society in the small town. Always, he would slip away with a keen sense of loss and shame burning in his heart.

Burning with anger over Meiling's humiliation, he wanted to rush forward and beat back the bullies who dared to hurt this girl. Although he was as strong as an ox, he was greatly outnumbered. He could only stand and watch in the shadows. As the crowd of students retreated, he moved forward, compelled by an inward anger that caused him to forget his low standing in life. He bent over and retrieved the torn and dirtied remnants of Meiling's books. Every eye seemed to be on him as he hesitantly approached her. He hardly dared to look her in the eye, but summoning every ounce of courage, he simply said, "I am truly sorry those ruffians frightened you and ruined your books." His eyes met hers for one brief moment as she shakily thanked him for his kindness.

He retreated as quickly as he had acted, his heart beating wildly. She had spoken to him! Even though she only said, "Oh, thank you very much. You are so kind," he would always remember the tenderness of her voice and the lovely eyes that smiled through her tears. Life had taken a sudden and unexpected turn, and he was happy.

Anching was never anxious to enter the halls of the school where so many shunned him and frequently poked fun at his cheap clothes, but today was different. Yesterday, the girl he admired so much had spoken to him. Never in his wildest imagination did he believe she would ever speak to him again. He was talking with a small group of other boys from the working class when he had the uncanny sensation that every eye in the group was fixed on something behind him. Turning slowly, he looked right into the eyes of Meiling. He felt the tingle of blood rush to his face at this unexpected encounter. She reached out and touched his sleeve as he turned, and said, "Anching, thank you so much for your kindness to me yesterday. I will never forget how courageously you acted and what a gentleman you were!"

Speechless, he simply nodded and gulped, as she quickly moved on her way through the crowd of students. Noticing the rising color in his face, his friends slapped him on the back in mock praise. "Hero!" one said with a hearty chuckle. "Now don't let this go to your head," another chimed in. "You're still Wen Anching, one of the poor guys of this school." "Yeah, and don't forget us now that the principal's daughter comes up and speaks to you," chided another. Everyone was enjoying Anching's embarrassment to the fullest.

"Ah, come on you guys," Anching replied softly, "I just did the right thing by picking up her books."

Fortunately for Anching, the bell rang and everyone drifted off to their classes. There were no more encounters with the beautiful Meiling, but the memory of the touch of her hand on his sleeve could not be erased from his mind. How he longed to feel that touch again. His life had been full of misery and poverty. His father, a hard working factory worker at the big plastics factory in town, had little time to be a real father. Long twelve-hour shifts seven days a week warped his life and separated him from everything beautiful and socially uplifting. He provided as well as he could for his large family, but life was rugged and tough, and every member of the family understood the sting of poverty and social ostracism. His mother was a good woman, but bowed down with years of struggling to make ends meet, of raising a large family on a pittance, and of being shoved around by those above her socially. They were a poor family. No one disputed that.

The fall festival was a great time for Puyang, when rich and poor alike sought some relief from the rigors of daily life. It was the occasion when the local gods from the temple were paraded through the streets to the beat of drums and shouts of people. It was also the time to feast on some delicacies sold by the local vendors at their little stands. Many drowned their sorrows in a drunken stupor that left them sick and more destitute than ever. Yet, year after year, they came and celebrated the harvest festival and thanked the gods for whatever harvest they enjoyed.

Several schools located in the surrounding villages near Puyang sent their best students to participate in the speech contest Principal Woo organized each year. His school always took the lead and often walked away with the prizes. This year, Anching was encouraged by his teacher to write a speech that would exalt the characteristics of courage and bravery in the face of insurmountable obstacles. Being an outstanding student, he hoped against all odds that he would be selected to represent the school.

But there was one obstacle in his way—Luping, son of the rich factory owner. He also wrote an essay, knowing full well that as usual he would be selected as the school's representative, based entirely on his rank as the son of the most powerful industrialist in town. It didn't take long for the confrontation between the rich man's son and the peasant boy to become a huge issue for the faculty. Although Anching was new in the school, he was by far the better student and his essay proved it. However, most of the teachers advised that it was better to play it safe and select Luping. After all, his father made a sizable annual contribution to the school, and all the teachers profited by higher salaries. Anching might have the better essay, but he was from one of the poorest families and he was in the school only because of the largess of the industrialist.

Principal Woo, himself a man of character, urged that the person who wrote the best essay be chosen. It did not require any modern means of communication for the upheaval to reach the ears of Luping's father. Nor did it take very long for him to make an unscheduled visit to Principal Woo's office. Stomping haughtily into the office, he demanded an explanation. How could the son of a poor factory worker who had no social standing in the community be considered before his son? How could Principal Woo allow such humiliation to the one who made the largest contribution to the school each year? He pressed his point home relentlessly, and ended with a threat. Either his son would be chosen or he would immediately withdraw his support. In fact, he backed it up by flipping a check on the desk for 10,000 yuan! "Take it, or leave it," he said with venom in his voice. "It is my son and the 10,000 yuan or the factory worker's son and no check, now or in the future!" He stormed out of the office, flinging open the door with a bang and striding arrogantly out of the building to his waiting car.

Stunned by the confrontation, Principal Woo sat silently at his desk, head bowed, in deep thought. It had always been a foregone conclusion that Luping would represent the school, and because he was a good speaker, he frequently brought home the prize. This year was different. Anching had clearly prepared the better speech, and by rights, should be selected. But even Principal Woo understood the politics of Puyang and the generous contributions Mr. Pang made each year. He recognized that his teachers were also willing to look the other way since it meant more in their pockets.

Principal Woo's conscience pulled him in one direction, but the practicality of the situation drove him back in the other direction. Sighing deeply, he picked up the check on his desk, rose slowly, and walked to the school treasurer. "Deposit this to our account," and then he walked away with bowed head and heavy heart.

Anching heard of the decision shortly before school was dismissed. Shattered by the news, he quickly left the building by a back door to avoid meeting Luping standing in a prominent place, smiling his smug smile of victory.

Walking swiftly, Anching quickly made his way to a secluded spot along the river where he often retreated to be alone to ponder his many problems. Reaching his favorite spot under a big dragon spruce tree, he flopped down on a rock and buried his face in his hands. Alone, he could weep. The hot tears coursed down his cheeks. *How unfair life is,* his heart screamed. *What a curse to be poor,* he wailed inwardly.

Suddenly, he sensed he was not alone. Lifting his head, he instinctively turned in the direction of the slight rustling sound behind him. Shocked, he quickly brushed the tears from his eyes as he stared into the face of Meiling.

"Forgive me for following you," she said quietly. "I couldn't help it. You were dealt a horrible blow of injustice and I am very angry with my father for what he has done to you. I watched you leave the school by the back door," she said with quavering voice. "Forgive me for following you to this beautiful spot."

Recovering his composure, Anching quickly rose to his feet, his school cap gripped tightly in his hand. No one of her rank ever spoke to him like this! The pounding of his heart was like the pounding of the temple drum. He feared she would hear it and run away. A thousand thoughts flashed through his mind as he gazed into her tear-filled eyes. *She is crying,* he realized, *but why?* A long black braid from either side drooped over her shoulders, framing her face. The picture was indelibly impressed on his memory. Years from now, he would think back to this magic moment and long to look into those eyes again. He was certain he had never seen a more beautiful sight, and he fumbled for the right words to express the whirling thoughts in his mind.

After what seemed like eternity, he bowed slightly and said, "Oh, please, you don't need to apologize. I hurried to this favorite spot to be alone, to ponder the events of today."

"May I sit here with you a little while?" she asked tentatively. "I know your heart must be bursting with sadness and disappointment."

"Oh, please sit here," he said with an embarrassed motion of his hand to the rock he had been sitting on. "It is not an elegant place to speak with a lady," he continued, gaining more confidence and composure, "but it is a beautiful, quiet spot where I find healing and comfort."

She brushed the tears from her eyes as she said, "Anching, I think you are the bravest man I have ever met."

He turned and gazed steadily into her eyes as he relished every word she spoke. "I do not deserve such praise, Meiling," he said sincerely. "I am only the son of a poor factory worker . . ."

As he took a breath to continue, he was shocked as she vehemently interrupted him saying, "You're not just the son of a poor factory worker! You are the son of a hard-working man who is honest, who puts his life in danger every day in that factory to provide for his family. He is proud of you, and so am I!"

The color rose in his face as he dropped his gaze and stared at the ground.

"Thank you," he mumbled. "My clothes are not as good as many of the students in our school, and I live in a very lowly house near the factory. Many times I feel that I don't belong here at all. I'm from a different world," he stammered.

"You have nothing to be ashamed of. You have an exceptional mind; not like that dim-witted Luping who bullies everyone around because his father is rich and owns the factory. All my friends know he is not half the student you are!" she said firmly as she flashed her beautiful smile.

Anching stood gazing into her eyes as he slowly said, "No one has ever made me feel like this before. You have treated me as an equal. Why do you speak like this?"

Meiling moved over and motioned for him to sit beside her, "Please sit here, and I will tell you why."

Meiling's invitation to sit next to her caught him off guard. His heart was again pounding so loudly, he was sure she could hear it. He dared not sit next to her. Instead he squatted at her side, relishing this wonderful moment.

She began to speak softly. "Many people consider that I am very privileged to be the daughter of Principal Woo. He is regarded in this community as a great educator and a very kind man. He has provided well for his family, and we are a very contented family. My mother often says we should be very thankful that the gods have smiled upon us." Meiling paused, and turning to look at Anching, she continued, "But there is something wrong in our family. We live for today, and we fear what will happen tomorrow. There is no purpose in living, and the future is so dark and hopeless."

Anching turned and looked at her in surprise. "I would never have imagined that anyone with your privileges and position in life could possibly feel as I do. I thought my poverty and low position in life was the root of all my problems. Do you feel empty inside like I do?" he asked incredulously.

"Well, not always," she answered honestly. "You see, something is happening to me. For several weeks, I have been slipping off to a gathering of young people at the church near the shoe factory."

"A church?" he exclaimed in surprise. "I thought churches were for the foreigners living in our city. I have heard that they spread corrupt ideas about China."

"That's what I thought also," she replied, "but a friend invited me to attend, and to my surprise, I have discovered that a strange and wonderful sense of peace comes into my heart as I listen to the pastor speak about the true and living God who loves me. He also speaks about Jesus Christ, God's Son, who loved everyone in the world so much that He even died on a cross to forgive us of our sin. He encourages the people to confess their sin to this Jesus, and to bring their sorrow and their problems to Him. The first time I attended, he gave me a book called *The Gospel of John* which tells the story of Jesus and what He did for the people of the world."

"And, is it better than the teachings of China's great teacher, Confucius?" he questioned in surprise. "His teachings have guided

China for centuries. He taught the great principles for living peacefully with our fellow men."

"There is something very different about this Jesus," she responded. "Confucius taught us to live right, but he never taught us how to live that way. This Jesus came to tell us how we could live differently. The pastor says when anyone invites Jesus to take control of his life, He actually comes to live within that person and helps him live differently."

"And have you invited this Jesus into your life, Meiling? Is that why you are so different from any other person I have ever known?"

She bowed her head and stared at the ground for a long minute. "I am searching for the answer to life," she said quietly, "but I have not yet found what I am looking for. I am interested in Jesus, and I read *The Gospel of John* every day, but I have not invited Jesus to take control of my life. If I became a Christian, my father would be very angry. He is a very good man, and he has high principles, but he is opposed to this foreign religion. You see, when he attended university in America, he learned a lot about Christianity, but he says he did not find reality in people's lives. They seemed to speak about moral things, but their lives did not measure up to their talk. He could not accept such a religion."

"And do you not find the same thing in this church?" he asked solemnly.

"Although they seem to talk about the same Jesus, I find these people not only claim to be changed within, but they actually give evidence of that change."

"Really?" Anching said with great interest. "You mean, you have met people who have changed their lifestyle?"

"That's exactly what I mean," she answered softly. "The people speak of God living in them, and giving them peace. They tell of answers to prayer and help with the everyday situations of life. One man told about this new power helping him to be free from the bondage of alcohol. Another woman told how she was able to overcome a very bad temper that caused much trouble in her home. Actually, I am really impressed by these testimonies of the change that happened within them. Although I have not invited Jesus into my life, I feel like my life already has some direction and purpose, and there is a sense of wonderful peace beginning to fill my heart."

"You are different than anyone else I have ever met," Anching responded honestly as he looked searchingly into her beautiful eyes. Something stirred within him. He could not explain it, but he longed to be like her, and he longed to stay in her presence forever!

"Maybe you would like to go with me sometime and see for yourself," she replied hesitantly.

He thought for a very long moment. He could not believe his ears. This lovely girl was inviting him to go with her to a meeting at a church! *It would be another opportunity to be with her,* he thought, but rising above the emotions of his heart, he realized that what he really wanted was the peace she spoke about. She was talking about something that seemed forever out of his reach: peace and forgiveness.

"I couldn't do that," he finally stammered. "I don't have clothing that is suitable to wear to such an occasion," he said flatly.

Meiling reached out impulsively and touched his sleeve while looking directly in his eyes. "Listen to me," she said firmly. "The pastor talks about eternal life, and he says God does not accept us because of our clothes, or good works. He accepts us because we are willing to follow and obey Him."

"I don't have any money to go to church," he whispered softly.

"Oh, Anching, no one needs money to go to this meeting. It is open to everyone without cost," she bubbled joyfully. "There are all kinds of people in the meeting. Most of the young people are dressed like you. You would not feel alone or out of place. In fact, your heart would stir with a strange warmth when they begin to sing."

"They sing?" he asked in surprise. "What do they sing about? What is there to sing about, really?"

"That's the amazing thing. When I am there, I want to sing even though my heart is breaking and heavy most of the time. They sing about God and His love and compassion for the people of the world. It is so different than the worship at the temple. Oh, you must come and hear it," she said with enthusiasm.

"When is the next meeting?" he asked with growing interest.

"Tomorrow night at seven o'clock. If you would like to attend, why not meet me at school about 6:15. It only takes about twenty minutes to reach the church from there. Will you do that? You will not be sorry, I promise."

"Tomorrow night," he answered, "I'll meet you at school. You know, I feel better already. This started out to be the worst day of my life, but you have changed all that. Thanks so much."

Meiling stood. "I must go," she said softly. "I'm glad I followed you."

"And so am I," he answered with a lilt in his voice.

He didn't fall asleep for a long time that night. He was amazed at his newfound friendship with Meiling, and what she had shared. What was this gospel book all about? Would it have answers to his heart cry for peace? He fell asleep more contented than any night in his memory.

Anching was not prepared for the inevitable meeting with Luping. He was standing in the middle of a group of his rich friends as Anching moved closer to the wall to pass them. Luping stepped out to block his way. Raising his voice in mock sympathy, he said loudly, "So sorry, Anching, that you came in second in the contest.

I am surprised that you had the ability to even come near me. Are you sure you did not copy someone else's speech?"

Luping's friends laughed, and added other derogatory remarks that cut deeply into Anching's heart. Lifting his head high, he replied for all to hear, "Luping, I worked very hard on my speech. It was all mine. Not one word was copied. I spoke the truth from my heart. Now the contest is over, and you have been selected as the winner. I congratulate you on your success."

Moving closer to the wall, he attempted to go on his way, but Luping and his friends blocked his passage. "So you thought you could write a better speech than mine," he chided. "How could a poor factory worker's son think he could compete with me? I have delivered the speech at this festival for the past three years. Everyone knows it's my right, and mine alone," he said with a smirk. "How did you have the nerve to challenge my place in the festival?" he asked haughtily.

Anching felt the blood rising in his neck. His fists clenched. He knew he could throw one blow and knock this nasty fellow to the ground. He could easily whip him thoroughly. Rage was rising as Luping continued to taunt him.

"So, you're ready to fight me right here in the school hall, are you?" he taunted as Anching took a step in his direction with upraised arms ready to fight. The loud voices attracted a growing crowd as Luping's friends continued to egg both of them on. Quite unexpectedly, the crowd parted as Meiling approached the two about to exchange blows. She looked with piercing eyes directly at Luping as he backed away with his friends lined up behind him.

"Luping," she said distinctly, as a deathly silence settled over the crowd, "you are a disgrace to our school. Everyone knows that it is your father's money that buys you the privilege to represent our school each year at the festival. It is not your intelligence that earns you the privilege. If you depended on brains you would end up last!" She spoke defiantly as the crowd of common students tittered with delight. The tense situation was about to explode into chaos when a teacher approached and ordered everyone to move on to their classes. Anching just stood there astonished as Meiling moved on to her class. *There will be serious consequences to this rash act,* he thought.

The battle lines had been drawn. The principal's daughter had defied the rich man's son.

Chapter 2

THE CONFRONTATION

Shortly after lunch break, a very angry Mr. Pang strode into Principal Woo's office demanding that Anching be expelled from school for humiliating his son in front of other students. "Mr. Pang," began Mr. Woo, "let's sit down and talk." He spoke quietly, trying to placate the angry man. "The teacher in charge reported everything to me immediately. The incident of our overzealous young people was unfortunate, but remember, your son was awarded first place in the contest and he will represent the school at the festival," he said with resignation in his voice. "Now, may I suggest that we drop the matter right there?" But it was only with a great amount of skillful persuasion that he was able to placate the irate factory owner.

As Meiling entered her home, her mother pulled her aside and whispered softly in her ear, "Your father is waiting to see you," she said apprehensively. "Meiling, please be careful. He is very angry."

Mr. Woo was sitting in a comfortable chair sipping tea when Meiling approached saying, "Father, I understand you want to see me."

He set his cup down and looked at his lovely daughter for a long moment. Then clearing his throat, he said, "Meiling, I have heard all the details of this morning's incident in which you placed me and the school at great risk of losing the financial support of Mr. Pang." Continuing to look intently at her, he continued, "This could have had very serious ramifications for you and for me. In the future, you must control yourself. Do you understand?" he asked sternly.

"Yes, father," she said humbly. "I did not mean to cause you any trouble, but Luping is always looking for trouble, and he always picks on Anching. Forgive me for stepping in this morning."

Looking at his pretty daughter, he said with a softening look on his face, "Meiling, that proud Pang boy had it coming to him!" He broke into a wide smile as he motioned Meiling to sit down. "Actually, I applaud your courage even though it created a very difficult situation. Be careful in the future or it might not turn out so well." He paused as he continued to admire his precious daughter. "But tell me, I have noticed something different about you recently. What has happened to you," he asked with keen interest, "that would cause you to step in to defend a poor factory worker's son? That seems most unusual."

She drew a deep breath, knowing that this would be a greater test than having stepped into the fray earlier in the day.

"Father," she started respectfully, "let me speak of Anching first. He may be a poor factory worker's son, but you know, as I do, that he is an excellent student who deserved to win the contest. I am very sorry that Mr. Pang's money was the deciding factor. Anching may be poor, but he is a man of courage and character, and I like that."

Mr. Woo rubbed his chin thoughtfully as he observed his daughter, "You're right, Meiling. He is a fine student, and I wish I could have granted him the honor of representing our school, but our school could not afford to pay our teachers the salaries they receive without Mr. Pang's generous contributions. I am sorry that I disappointed you, but under the circumstances, I had no other alternative."

"I know these are perilous times," she replied, "and that brings me to the second part of your question. My heart is so heavy because our lives are only filled with hopelessness and despair that cause us to do things only to make ourselves more comfortable. But life has no purpose, no goals. The future is so uncertain, and your lot as an intellectual is very precarious should the Communist insurgency succeed. When my friend invited me to attend a Christian meeting sometime ago, I only went out of curiosity. I did not believe there could be answers there."

Mr. Woo sat bolt upright in his chair as if struck by lightning. He looked at his daughter with piercing eyes. "You know I object to this foreign religion. It is not Chinese. It is not for us," he said emphatically, glaring at her.

"That's what you taught me, Father," she replied courteously, "but I discovered a peace there that I have not found anywhere else. Life has begun to have new purpose and meaning since I have been reading the words of Jesus in the Gospel of John. I wish you too would read it. I believe it has some answers for all of us in these days of war and bloodshed."

Stunned, Mr. Woo sat staring at his daughter for several long minutes. "What have you heard that makes you think this foreign religion can help us Chinese?"

For the next hour, Meiling patiently explained all she had heard and read. Her father listened with unusual attention and without the usual rancor that always accompanied his protests against Christianity.

"Your mother and I are facing some great uncertainties, and possibly death, should the Communists succeed in overthrowing the government," he said slowly. "They do not look with favor on intellectuals, especially those educated in the west. The reports from the north do not offer us much hope," he said with deep despair. "There are hard times ahead of us. Maybe I need to look into this more carefully," he said as he placed his arm around his beloved daughter. "We will talk again," he said as they walked toward the kitchen.

Meiling explained to her mother that she was meeting some friends and attending a very important meeting. "Are you going to the church again?" she asked simply. "I overheard your conversation with your father. I too, have had that empty feeling inside of me all my life. Tell me more when you return," she said with a smile and a loving pat on her arm.

Meiling walked briskly to the school to meet Anching, hardly able to believe what had transpired. She saw him before he noticed her approaching. Her heart quickened as she looked at this strong, handsome young man who came from a poor family, but who possessed all the qualities of character she hoped for in a man. Hearing her footsteps, Anching turned and saw her face aglow with joy and excitement. His heart beat faster as he watched her, and then a sobering thought gripped him. *I'm a nobody. I'm from a different world.*

"Anching," she said excitedly, "you won't believe what happened to me this afternoon! My father was waiting for me when I returned home, and I fully expected to be severely reprimanded for this morning's actions. Instead, he actually supported what I did! He said Luping had it coming to him! Can you imagine that?"

Without giving him time to respond, she bubbled on. "And besides that, I have the most wonderful news to share with you. In response to my father's question as to why I seem to have changed so much, I told him about the church and the Gospel of John I have been reading. I fully expected him to rise up and sternly forbid me to attend another meeting. Instead, we talked for almost an hour about what I am learning. He even expressed a desire to read the gospel."

Catching the enthusiasm in her voice, he smiled broadly as they walked briskly to the church.

"And your father did not scold you for talking to me?" he asked incredulously.

"He told me he respected you very much, and only wished he could have given you the honor of representing our school. He asked me to try and understand that Mr. Pang is a powerful figure in our community, and he makes generous contributions to our school that enables him to pay better salaries to the teachers."

"And your father did not reprimand you for associating with me?" he asked again incredulously.

"Not one word of rebuke. In fact, I think he likes you very much."

"Now that's a miracle," he said with a satisfied smile.

Their animated conversation made the walk seem like nothing at all. *What is it,* they both thought to themselves, *that makes life so exciting when we are together?* Entering the church, Anching took notice that fifty or sixty young people had already arrived, and they were chatting with much animation and joy. Meiling introduced him around to these new friends. Strange, everyone seemed to welcome him with such sincerity. None looked down on him for his simple clothes. He began to relax and feel like he belonged in this group.

As the pastor announced the first hymn and the group began to sing, Anching's heart began to melt. He read the unfamiliar words and listened intently to the tune which was very foreign to him.

What a friend we have in Jesus, all our sins and griefs to bear,
What a privilege to carry, everything to God in prayer.

The students continued singing, but he was lost in thought. Could it be true that someone called God really cared about him? The bigger question that flooded his mind was, *Did this God really know he was alive? Was He someone who was really interested in all his grief and sins?* By the time he was roused from these thoughts, the students had started singing the third verse of the hymn.

Are we weak and heavy laden, cumbered with a load of care?
Precious Savior, still our refuge—Take it to the Lord in prayer.
Do your friends despise, forsake you? Take it to the Lord in prayer:
In His arms he'll take and shield you. You will find a solace there.

Never in his life had he heard anything like that. His heart was moved with a sense of peace he never expected to feel. He listened intently to every word the pastor spoke.

"Brothers and sisters," he began.

What about the rich and famous? thought Anching. *He called us all brothers and sisters without reference to position or rank.* He guardedly glanced around the room. Obviously, they were all students. Most were dressed as he was; only a few showed signs of better clothes, yet everyone sat together, hanging on to every word the pastor spoke. *I must pay attention and not let my thoughts wander like this,* he thought. *I am missing too much!* The pastor continued speaking about what it meant to be a follower of Jesus. He spoke of the cross where Jesus died for everyone in the world regardless of rank or race, simply because He loved everyone so much and wanted to give them eternal life.

Now he was talking about the cost of following Jesus. *Ah, yes, here it is at last,* he thought. *I knew there was a catch somewhere. It was going to cost something, and I have nothing to offer!*

"My dear young people," continued the pastor, "Jesus invites everyone to follow Him without cost. All the money in the world could never buy the peace He offers as a free gift.

"Believe me," he said with confidence and excitement, "salvation is through Jesus Christ alone, and it is truly a free gift. All one needs to do is to come to Him and confess he is a sinner, and receive His full pardon. At that very moment, you receive eternal life.

"But, let me add, that when you follow Jesus, there will be a price to pay as people ridicule you, and as our great enemy, Satan, tries to deceive you and hold you back. Be strong in the Lord, and depend on His Word, the Bible, to strengthen you each day. Then no matter what happens in life, Jesus will be there to help you through."

Some heads were nodding in agreement, and some were smiling. One young man raised his hand and asked if he might say something.

"Of course," responded the pastor. "You must have a testimony you want to give."

"I do," replied the young man. "Just today, my uncle arrived from north China. The Communists have occupied his area and have begun to impose their new regulations on the community. They seem to have forgotten their promises to make us all happy and fill our rice bowls. My uncle told of the small church in his community that was shut down one night right in the middle of the service. Soldiers burst into the room, and shouting Mao slogans, they ordered the people to stand against the walls of the church."

"Who is the pastor? a soldier shouted.

"I am," said an older man quietly as he stepped forward. "What is the meaning of this interruption?"

The surly soldier walked up to him and slapped him across the face and said, "You do not address an officer of the People's Republic with such impudence. We ask the questions, you obey. We have come tonight to inform you that the People's Republic needs this building for the people's use. No more meetings will be held here. Foreigners and their superstitious religion have duped you into following this Jesus. You must give up these false beliefs and follow Chairman Mao or else you will suffer the consequences."

Every eye in the room was riveted on the young man as he continued. "My uncle reported that the pastor was handcuffed in front of the people and rudely pushed out the door. As the congregation stood trembling and in absolute silence, the soldier ordered harshly, 'Now leave, and don't come back here again. The people's army will use this building from now on.' It was three weeks before the pastor returned," he continued. "My uncle reported that the pastor showed them his back was cut and bruised from many beatings with bamboo strips. His wrists showed wounds from handcuffs that were left on his hands day and night. He reported being tortured by being denied sleep and water. Day after day they tried to force him to write confessions that stated he was a lackey of the American imperialists and a traitor to China.

"The pastor reported that the prison guards gave him several sheets of paper to write out his confession. All he was expected to do was to renounce Jesus and the imperialists. When he refused, he was beaten again and again. He refused to give up his faith in Jesus Christ."

The students sat transfixed. Anching wondered, *Why would anyone endure such treatment and pain for this foreign God? Who is He, that this pastor would endure punishment day after day, and refuse to sign the documents that would have set him free?*

"My uncle reported an amazing thing," the student continued. "He reported that the number of believers has more than doubled since this incident. The people are meeting secretly in homes in different parts of the city while the pastor moves from one home to another. I was amazed to hear him say that he is filled with joy because he had the privilege of suffering for Jesus. Pastor, I think that is what you have been teaching us tonight," he said as he sat down.

Everyone in the room sat spellbound. The pastor looked around and said, "Dear students, this is an example of the cost of following Jesus, but I want each of you to know that it is worthwhile. Jesus gives eternal life and no one can rob us of that hope. These same circumstances may happen to us in this area some day if the Communists continue to win the battle. We must determine to be strong in the Lord and press on, regardless of the cost."

He closed the meeting with a prayer for strength and courage. He prayed that each one would open his heart to Jesus and find His peace. Then it was over and the students milled around, talking quietly. No one was in a hurry to leave. Anching wished it would never end. He had never felt this way in his whole life, and he hated to break the spell.

As he and Meiling walked quietly back to the school, they were both in deep thought, considering the cost of following Jesus. As they neared the school, Meiling broke the silence. "I read this morning the words of Jesus in the little book," she volunteered. "It said that Jesus offers eternal life to all who believe, but for those who reject His gift, there is nothing but eternal death. I think that pastor who was beaten so savagely must believe that the eternal life Jesus offers is worth more than the promises of the Communists."

"The thought that struck me," replied Anching, "is that this must be worth dying for. If that is not true, then why would anyone endure such beatings and loss of property?"

"I think I know the answer to that," Meiling responded. "Jesus said in the gospel that He was preparing a place for all who believed in Him, and one day He would come and take them to be with Him. I think that means that in the life to come there is hope even though there may be trouble and death in this one."

"But that is a big 'if,' don't you think?" he asked softly. "Suppose it is not true? Suppose it is only a dream? Then what?"

"I don't know," she replied honestly, "but I have heard that there are hundreds and hundreds of believers who have been willing to die for Jesus. Do you think so many would die for a lie?"

"I guess not," he replied. "Tonight I will begin reading this Gospel of John the pastor gave me. You seem to find much hope and joy in Jesus' words. Maybe I will also."

Arriving at the school entrance, Anching paused a moment, and then asked simply, "May I walk you to your home? It is already quite dark. I would feel better knowing that you are safely in your home."

It was too dark for him to see the flush that rose in her face as she replied, "Oh, thank you very much. I know my mother would be pleased to have you do that."

His heart skipped a beat as he said, "Then let's go on." At the entrance to her home, he paused and said, "Meiling, thank you for all you have done for me, and thank you for inviting me to attend the meeting. I have so much to think about. I hope we can go again."

"The next meeting is on Sunday morning," she replied. "It is a little different because many people, both young and old attend. The singing and preaching is very uplifting. I hope you will go with me. Good night, Anching."

"Good night," he answered quietly, "I will never forget today as long as I live."

One afternoon as the two sat together by the riverside, Meiling hesitantly began to open her heart with her concerns for her father.

"My father is very restless these days," she began. "The rumors from the occupied areas in the north are very disturbing. I overheard him talking to my mother the other night as he shared the latest reports about intellectuals and capitalists in the occupied areas. Apparently, the Communists lump landowners, intellectuals, and capitalists, and even Christians, all together and consider them enemies of the state."

Anching noticed that her hands trembled as she spoke. "Those reports must be very unnerving to your father and to you," he said sympathetically.

"An old school friend of father's escaped the area and made his way south," she continued. "He told my father that all teachers, and especially principals, were subjected to humiliating and often very painful experiences in what they call 'struggle meetings.'"

"And what does that mean?" he asked with growing interest.

"According to my father's friend, he reported that 'struggle meetings' are horrible meetings where people are forced to attend and testify against whoever is being tried by the Communist tribunal. Several pre-selected people make false accusations against the person, and repeat accusations that have been rehearsed. The trials are rigged and no defense is allowed whatsoever. Sentence is passed by a small panel of judges. Father's friend reported being forced to watch victims being severely beaten, and on one occasion, the person was actually beaten to death."

"You mean that the person charged has no access to a lawyer, and no opportunity to make a defense?" he asked in shocked surprise.

"Father says that's the way the Communists control the people. They use the weapon of fear and the people do anything to save their own lives."

"And how does he think that will affect his family?" he asked with concern.

"My father is very concerned because he is an intellectual. He will be one of the first to suffer," he says.

"It will never work here in our school," Anching declared vehemently. "People are too loyal to your father to do anything to hurt him."

"Oh, how I wish that were true. Father warned my mother that should he be put on trial in a 'struggle meeting,' no one will dare oppose the Communists. People do strange things when their own lives are threatened. I heard my father say, if we stay, we'll die, and if we flee we're apt to die. My parents wept together a long time and so did I."

"I didn't realize conditions were as terrible as that," he answered solemnly. Then as he paused, a shocking thought flashed into his mind. "If your parents fled this area, that would include you, too, wouldn't it?" he asked with fear clutching his throat. Without waiting for an answer, he blurted out, "Oh, Meiling, I don't know what I would do if you were to leave here," he confessed.

Shocked by these unexpected words prompted by the deep feelings of emotion welling up in his heart, he just sat there petrified. *What will she think of such a confession?* he thought. *Will she leave me now and never speak to me again? I have broken all the rules of Chinese etiquette!* He dared not look at her lest he see the disapproval in her eyes. Silence reigned for a few moments as he sat stunned and frightened at his possible loss.

A surge of relief flooded his heart as he heard her say, "Oh, Anching, during these last few days, I have realized that you have become such an important part of my life. I, too, feel that life would not be worth living without you!"

He stole a furtive glance at her. Tears were welling up in her eyes.

Encouraged, he said, "You mean so much to me. Someday when I have gained a college degree and have found a good job, I hope you will consent . . ." He paused as fear gripped his heart.

What am I saying, he thought anxiously. *I really have been carried away with emotion. How did I ever dare to voice such a thought! She will surely turn her back on me, the poor factory worker's son, and I will lose her forever!*

His anxious thoughts subsided as she reached out and touched his arm, saying, "Anching, I would wait forever for you," she said simply as the tears coursed down her cheeks.

Both were suddenly conscious of their embarrassment at the revelation of their deep emotion for each other, and the profound meaning of this moment.

"The future may look dismal at this moment," he replied huskily as he fought back his emotions, "but I will study and work as diligently as possible to be worthy of you."

They sat quietly for a few minutes watching the lazy river flow by. Both were lost in deep thought as they contemplated the dangers of the future. Had they known what was soon to transpire, they would have fled the spot to find refuge somewhere from the coming storm.

Then, a bright thought flashed into Meiling's mind. "I haven't told you yet that after hearing my parents talking the other night, I felt so desperately sad and helpless. It was then that I prayed and asked Jesus to come into my life. I felt I needed Him more than anything else in the entire world at that moment. As I prayed, a wonderful peace settled on my heart and it seemed that my room was lit with a brilliant light. I thought Jesus was standing right there by my side with open arms to receive me. Oh, Anching, it was the most beautiful thing that ever happened to me."

A beautiful smile made the tear-stained cheeks glow with such beauty, he knew this was very real.

"I'm so glad to hear that," he responded reverently. "I wish I could tell you that I have done the same thing. But there are still so many unanswered questions in my heart. I hope some day I can find this same peace," he said with sincerity.

"Oh, you will, you will," she responded joyfully. "In God's time, you will! Just be faithful in reading the Bible and attending church. God will lead you along step by step just as He led me. I pray for you every day without fail."

Anching looked at her. "For a poor factory worker's son, I must be the most fortunate man on earth. To have you as my friend and to be treated as an equal amazes me. I know it must be Jesus at work in your life," he said with conviction. "I will continue to seek Him."

"Oh, it is getting late," she said as she jumped up to go. "I'll meet you tomorrow night for the meeting at church." With that she quickly slipped away and disappeared down the trail to the main road, but her presence lingered as he savored every sentence of their conversation. *She said she will wait for me forever!* The fountain of joy broke loose within his heart and he began to sing a song of joy he had learned at church.

One night at the church meeting, Pastor Yang explained the meaning and significance of baptism as the outward sign that Christ was reigning as Lord within. He invited those who wished to be baptized to join a special class on the coming Sunday before the worship service. The room buzzed with excitement as the students asked each other, "Are you going to be baptized?"

As they walked home, Meiling spoke. "I told you several weeks ago that I prayed and invited Jesus into my life. These have been the most exciting days of my life. I intend to be baptized and declare my faith publicly."

They walked on in silence for a few moments. Only the scuffing of their shoes could be heard as Meiling waited for some response.

"I think I would like to be baptized also," he said at last, "but I am still not sure who Jesus really is."

"I know, and I am praying for you," she responded.

"Thank you, Meiling, I am almost there, I think."

As they reached the gate of her home, she slipped inside. As the door closed, he continued looking up at the beautiful full moon, and then he spoke out loud. "Oh, God, if You are really alive, and if You are the only true God, prove it to me by answering my prayer, and I will believe. You know that every member of my family works hard to earn a few yuan, but still we are so poor. My father works in one of the most dangerous areas of the factory and earns such a small wage." He continued praying as he walked slowly toward his own humble home. "I want to know You as Meiling does. I am following Pastor Yang's advice when he said we should ask for Your help and watch You work. I am asking now, that You will give my father a new job in a less dangerous place with more pay. Then I will know that You are God, and I will follow You."

He stopped, and looked up at the starry sky. *What did I just pray? Was it right to ask such a request? Am I too bold? But wasn't that what the pastor instructed them to do a few minutes ago?*

It seemed as if he heard an audible voice behind him. *My son,* the voice sounded. *You are seeking Me. I will prove to you that I am the living God.*

Startled, he looked around. The voice was so clear; it was as if someone behind him had spoken. No one was there. He was alone in the street. *Was that the voice of God?* The words of the pastor came back to him. He had quoted the words of Jesus when He said, "If you ask anything in My name, it shall be done!" *That's what I just did.* A sweet sense of peace filled his troubled heart. He never remembered seeing the stars shine more brightly before and he never had such joy fill his heart.

A couple of days later when Anching's father returned home from work, there was such a commotion in the kitchen, he rushed out to see what it was all about. His father was speaking with such animation that he knew something unusual had happened. He was usually a man of few words, but today was different. *Had he been injured? Was there trouble at the factory? Had he lost his job?* These thoughts flooded Anching's mind as he tried to fathom what was happening.

"Family," his father fairly shouted. "Listen to this good news. This morning, Mr. Pang called me into his office. I entered with fear and trembling expecting I was about to be fired. To my surprise, he said, 'Wen, you have been a model worker here for many years. Your work is far superior to that of most of the people in this factory. I have decided to promote you to be head of your department starting immediately. Your salary will be increased to 25 yuan a week!'"

"Twenty-five yuan a week?" gasped Mrs. Wen. "Why, that is triple your present salary!"

Every member of the family had crowded around, unable to believe this unexpected good fortune that had come to their family. As the reality of the increased salary dawned on Mrs. Wen, she pulled her apron up to her eyes and sobbed for joy. Mr. Wen danced around the room in his excitement. Never had any of the children seen their parents express such joy and emotion before. When things quieted down a little, Mr. Wen explained that his new job would remove him from the dangerous machinery he had worked with every day for these many years.

"The gods are looking on us with good fortune," he said joyfully. Then, pausing, he looked at Anching and asked, "Or maybe it has something to do with you, Anching. I hear you have been attending the meetings of the foreign God. Have you been praying to Him about our family?" he asked inquisitively.

Anching froze in his tracks. He could hardly believe what his father was saying. *How did he know about his interest in Jesus?* He had never spoken a word to him about the church or his growing faith. It must have been his mother. *I told her about the meetings and the Gospel of John.* He remembered her many questions and the spiritual hunger she had expressed as he told her about the pastor's sermons. Suddenly, he remembered his prayer under the stars a couple of nights ago. The words of his prayer flashed back into his mind. *If You are God, give my father a new position in a less dangerous place and with higher pay, and I will believe.*

Every eye focused on him at that moment. The room swirled and he felt dizzy. His father had always opposed the foreigner's religion just as all good Chinese did. *What would be his reaction?* Everyone was well acquainted with his fiery temper and the consequences.

Hesitating a few moments, he calculated the risk of declaring his faith in Jesus and then he remembered the pastor saying that if anyone was ashamed of Jesus, He would be ashamed of that person. He opened his mouth to speak, but nothing came out.

"Come on son, speak up," his father commanded. "Did you pray to that foreign God about me and my job?"

Everyone was staring intently at Anching. They all had heard about the church. They all wondered what he would say, and what would be their father's reaction. Anching cleared his throat, and looking directly at his father, he told the family the whole story of his prayer. Stunned, they stood in absolute silence waiting for their father's reaction.

"And now what?" asked his father with piercing eyes. "You said you would follow this Jesus if He answered your prayer. Is that what you intend to do?" he probed.

Trembling, Anching slowly responded, his confidence growing as he spoke. "Father, I respect you very much and I will always honor you. I know you have never thought much about Jesus because you thought He was the foreigner's God. I have been seeking for peace in my heart, and until I heard of Jesus, there was nothing but fear and hopelessness. I did pray that you would get a different job at higher pay, and I said to God that if He answered my prayer, I would know He was the true and living God. He answered my prayer, and I will follow Him."

Everyone continued to gawk in awe at this unbelievable conversation taking place in their home. They expected the joyous occasion to turn to one of anger and shouting. They looked expectantly at their father. *Was that tears in his eyes?* They looked more closely. *Could it be true that there were really tears in their father's eyes?* No one had ever seen their father cry. A tear slipped down his cheek as he reached out to his son, and said, "You have always been a brave and strong young man of deep character and honesty," he choked. "Thank you for praying for me. Maybe this Jesus did answer your prayers. Maybe," he paused in deep thought, "maybe He is the true God after all."

Stunned by these remarks, it took a few moments for the significance of them to penetrate each mind. Suddenly, the room erupted with joy such as they had never experienced as a family before. Anching's heart was bursting. He had declared his faith in Jesus before his family, and unbelievably, his father was not angry. In fact, he went on to say that maybe they all ought to look into this book!

Chapter 3

TROUBLE BREWING

Pastor Yang was planning special meetings during the Chinese New Year holidays that usually fell in early February. All Chinese churches plan special meetings during this three-day holiday to give the believers an alternative to the Buddhist and other religious festivals. He had big plans for a joyful baptismal service that would be an historic milestone for the Puyang church.

"All over China," he said to his eager congregation, "Chinese are celebrating the coming of the new year. Most will invoke the favor of the gods and hope for a prosperous year. We Christians will gather together to worship the true and living God. We will simply seek first the kingdom of God. I am happy to announce that thirty-five people will publicly declare their faith in Jesus Christ as Savior and Lord in this service. We are all aware," he continued as he looked each of the candidates in the eye, "that the Communist army is continuing to advance southward. If they succeed in reaching Puyang, I want each of you to understand that there will be serious repercussions for Christians. It will probably mean that many of us will suffer for Jesus, and some will lay down their lives as martyrs. You must count the cost of following Jesus."

Every eye was fixed on him. No one moved as the consequences of surrender to Jesus sank in.

"I urge each person here tonight to consider these words very carefully. If you follow Jesus, He will give you eternal life, but nowhere does Scripture guarantee a life free from pain or suffering. Rather, we understand that to follow Jesus means we will suffer. Do you understand that, young people?" he asked earnestly. He paused to let his words penetrate their minds. The silence was deafening as each one searched his own heart.

Each one sat quietly reflecting on these words. The silence was broken as a young man hesitantly stood to his feet and said, "Pastor, I am not sure I want to take the risk."

Every head turned to see who had spoken. "The price is too high. I have a great ambition to make something of my life that will help our country and bring me security and even a comfortable living. If I follow Jesus as you say, the Communists may kill me. Isn't it possible to be a Christian and avoid the suffering you are speaking about?"

"My dear friend," the pastor said with sadness in his voice, "Jesus said we cannot serve God and this world system at the same time. We must love one and hate the other. If you choose to follow Jesus, you will suffer persecution under the Communists I am sure. You may even lose your life, but you will have gained something no one can take from you—eternal life. If you choose this world system with its promises of ease and security, you may gain them only for a very short time. In the end, you will suffer eternal separation from God. That is why I am spelling out the consequences. I cannot promise you a life of ease and wealth, but I can promise you eternal life in heaven. It is written here in the Gospel of John that whoever believes in Jesus has eternal life, and whoever does not believe, does not have life, but eternal death and separation from God."

The young man looked around at his friends with anguish etched on his face. Everyone felt the struggle in his heart. It caused them to search their own hearts and make a decision. Then with sorrow in his voice he slowly said, "Pastor, I have been helped by your sermons. They have lifted my troubled heart many times. I even said I wanted to be baptized." He paused, as the agitation on his face grew more pronounced. "Up until this moment I had intended to be baptized," he repeated, "but I cannot pay such a high price." He looked around once more at his friends, bowed his head, and slowly walked out of the room alone.

Tears trickled down the pastor's face as he said, "Young people, only you can make the decision to follow Jesus. If you do, He will never leave you nor forsake you, and in the midst of trials and suffering, He will be there to carry you through to glorious victory." He paused and looked earnestly into the faces of the people before him as he continued, "I plead with you to make the right choice. As for me, it may cost me imprisonment or even death, nevertheless, I will not turn my back on Jesus."

No one moved and not a sound could be heard as each contemplated the consequences of this moment. Suddenly, as if by one voice, a chorus of voices spoke in unison, assuring the pastor that they understood the cost, and they were prepared to follow.

"Praise God," he said as a big smile spread across his face. "You will never regret that decision. I am prepared to lay down my life for Jesus if necessary. He means everything to me."

A few days before the baptismal service, Mr. Woo led Meiling to a quiet spot in their home where he opened his heart and shared his concerns for their future under Communism.

"Meiling," he began very seriously, "you are about to take a very big step in life. I understand that you would like to be baptized on New Year's Day. Your mother also tells me that you would like us to be present. Is that right?"

"Yes, that's right, Father," she responded wondering where this conversation was headed.

"Meiling," he said gently, "I'm afraid that will not be possible." As disappointment showed in her downcast expression, he hastened to add, "but it is not because I object. The change that I have observed in you ever since you started attending the church is most remarkable. I have watched you more carefully than you realize, and I am very impressed." He paused and drew a deep breath. "However, we are living in very perilous times, and I believe, in the near future, unless there is a great miracle, our city will fall to the Communist army. When that happens, we will all suffer intensely."

He continued quietly, "I'm afraid the river will run red—red with the blood of millions of Chinese." He paused as if contemplating closing the conversation, then he added soberly, "You're aware of the 'struggle meetings' the Communists organize when they have gained control, and I think you're aware that intellectuals and capitalists come under severe criticism. In my case, as an educator, I will be one of the first to be condemned."

"Oh, Father, do you really believe that will happen in our city? And will you be tried like a criminal?" she said as she choked back the tears.

"My precious daughter," he said tenderly, "I do not see how I can escape. I have confided in your mother that sooner or later, they will come for me. I cannot begin to imagine what the end will be," he said quietly. "Without doubt, I will be a prime target, but if in addition to being an intellectual and principal of the school, they can charge me with supporting Christianity and the church meetings, it will be doubly hard for all of us."

"Oh, Father, I would never want to cause you any suffering. You have been a wonderful father to me, and I cannot bear the thought that you will be tried."

"There are many things we do not understand, and there are many things we will not be able to avoid, but one thing is certain. I will be a loyal Chinese until the bitter end."

Meiling wept hot, searing tears as the full implications of her father's words sank in.

"Do you think they will harm Mother also?" she asked apprehensively.

"My dear daughter, I am afraid that we will all suffer. You must be strong no matter what happens because some day freedom will once again come to our land. I will not see it, but you will. Since you have become a Christian, I have been comforted that the Jesus you speak of will somehow help you through the terrible bloodbath that is coming in our land."

"Oh, Father, I have been praying that you and Mother would find this same peace I have found, and experience God's free gift of eternal life. I understand why you will not be able to attend the baptismal service, but I am so happy that you do not object. Now, I only hope and pray that you will find Jesus as I have, because you will need His help when the trouble comes."

"I would like to read your Gospel of John, and perhaps you can tell me more about the teaching you receive at the church. I met Pastor Yang recently at a meeting, and I was deeply impressed with him. He, too, is facing some unspeakable experiences when the Communists come. I admire his courage so much."

"Pastor Yang has told us that," she replied sadly, "but he always says that Jesus is worth dying for and that he will never give up his faith in Him. He also warned us that to take the step of baptism may be very costly to us. That is why we are memorizing Bible verses that will strengthen us when the crisis comes."

"Meiling, you are a remarkably courageous girl. But are you not afraid that this step will bring disaster to you?"

"Yes, Father, I am afraid when I hear the reports from the north, but I have found such wonderful peace in Jesus that I could never turn my back on Him. With His help, I will be strong when the time comes," she said softly, little realizing how prophetic was this statement.

Mr. Woo looked long and deeply into the eyes of his daughter. *How I wish I could spare you the sorrow that is coming to China.* Then changing the subject, he shocked her by asking, "Would you give me the Gospel of John you have spoken about, and then some day, come and explain what you have learned about Jesus? I think it is time for your mother and me to think about these things."

Meiling fairly leaped with joy. "Oh, Father, let me get it for you right away. Read it with an open mind and you will discover the thrilling secret of peace with God."

She was about to dash off to get the gospel for him when he spoke. "I have heard rumors through your mother that you are very fond of this young man, Anching, and that you walk back and forth to church with him regularly. Is that correct?" he asked with a twinkle in his eyes.

Blushing with embarrassment, she bowed her head and said, "Father, Anching is a young man I admire very much. He has also become a believer and will be baptized. I wish you knew him better. You would like him very much," she replied without lifting her eyes.

"Yes, I should make it a point to know him better. Perhaps some day we could invite him to have dinner with us. Would you like that?" he asked with a chuckle. "I know China is really changing," he said, "and you and Anching are part of that change. I have the feeling that you two will affect China's future in a very significant way. Yes, let's invite him to dinner to celebrate your baptisms," he said as he embraced his daughter.

"Oh, thank you. Thank you," she said as she lifted her eyes to meet his. "That is the next best thing to having you attend the baptismal service."

"You are so much like your mother," he whispered as he looked into her eyes. "Just be careful. The times are very dangerous and I fear for you."

"I am afraid," she responded, "but Jesus has promised to be with me wherever I go and no matter what the circumstances may be. I will trust Him and not be afraid," she said softly.

"Good, and now why don't you let me see that book you think so much about? I better start reading it, or you and Anching will be way ahead of me," he said laughingly.

In the weeks that followed the baptismal service, Mr. Woo spent many an evening reading the Gospel of John. Captivated by its message, he bought himself a Bible and had long conversations with his daughter. Mrs. Woo, on the other hand, soon found herself attending the church where she drank in the truths Pastor Yang expounded. Mother and daughter found new hope and joy together.

The weeks passed quickly and graduation was fast approaching. By this time, Anching had established himself as the most outstanding young student in the school's history. He and Luping managed to avoid open conflict only because Anching studiously refused to be drawn into it. Luping was seething with jealousy and even hatred. He waited like a cat stalking a mouse, waiting to pounce when the opportunity arose.

One day in May, the city was astir with the news that a large contingent of government troops was approaching the city from the south. They would be passing through Puyang on their way north to engage the enemy forces. The news was met with trepidation because government troops often acted ruthlessly, and at times caused much pain and suffering. Supplies for the troops were always short, and that created many serious problems, and billeting was never adequate at the barracks. Consequently, hungry troops demanded food and housing from the people, and when it was denied them, they used force to obtain whatever they wanted.

"Will the troops occupy our school?" the teachers queried. "How long will they stay in our city?" they worried.

Mr. Woo had no answers, but he was filled with apprehension. Reports from the south indicated that the troops left behind a trail of havoc and sorrow. Citizens were robbed and buildings were vandalized. Besides, they were forcibly conscripting young men into the army at gunpoint.

A small advance unit of the army entered Puyang to scout out suitable places to billet the troops. Already it was like a ghost town. School had been dismissed, and only Mr. Woo and some male teachers were barricaded behind locked doors.

"Open up," shouted the leader of the unit as he pounded on the door. "We are going to need this building for three or four days."

Mr. Woo hesitated to open the door for fear of what was coming. The incessant pounding rattled the windows and the shouting increased as the impatient soldiers demanded entrance.

As the door opened a crack, the unit commander pushed in violently and rudely shoved past the startled Mr. Woo.

"What's the matter with you? Do you think we have forever?" he snarled as he stamped around the lobby area. "The troops will be here tomorrow at 9 A.M.," he continued shouting. "We will billet 100 men in here."

"But this is a school," protested Mr. Woo. "There is an army barracks in town that should be used by the troops."

"Are you denying the troops of the Chinese Army the right to rest here?" shouted the angry officer. "We are engaged in fighting the Communists. Every good Chinese should be willing to make the same sacrifices the men in the army are making," he bellowed.

"But what of the children?" questioned Mr. Woo.

"Give them a few days' vacation until we move on. We need a place to sleep," he replied, softening his remarks a little. "I promise we will not vandalize the building. We will need the school playground to prepare our food. You can help us by supplying us with firewood. I see you have a good supply on hand."

Seeing the questioning look on Mr. Woo's face, he continued, "And don't expect payment for it either. This is war, and everyone has to share in the cost."

Turning to his men, he motioned them out, thus ending any further protest. Deeply troubled at the turn of events, Mr. Woo slowly recovered as the army vehicle pulled away.

"We had better begin clearing these rooms of supplies," he said to his teachers. "Lock up everything you can and hope for the best."

The plastics factory also shut down as troops were to be billeted there as well. Even the small clinic was not excluded, although only the sick would be brought there for free treatment. The townspeople were reeling from the harsh orders. No one dared to object, though there was much grumbling as they all began to stash away their valuables and as much food as they could.

Early the next morning, the troops began arriving and took over the town. Talking loudly and pushing their way around, the contingent of 100 men burst into the school as each man was intent on staking out a spot for his bedding roll. It wasn't long until dozens of little cooking stoves were set up in the schoolyard and groups of men began preparing their rice for breakfast. Mr. Woo and his teachers stayed clear of the occupied area, but they maintained a watchful surveillance of everything.

"Stay out of sight as much as possible," he reminded his teachers, "but keep an eye on things. Let's hope for the best."

"These troops have been here for three days already," grumbled the people, "and they have stripped us of our rice and fuel. When will they be moving on?"

"This is devastating our community," complained the mayor angrily to the army major in charge. "How do you expect to win the loyalty of the people when you strip them of their food and possessions?"

"Our supplies should be arriving tonight," the leader soothed, "and then we will replace everything we have used from the townspeople."

To his aides, the mayor remarked ruefully, "I will believe that when I see it."

Early on the morning of the fourth day, soldiers pounded on village doors, ordering the young men at gunpoint to get into the waiting trucks.

Shouts could be heard everywhere. "What is this all about? Why are you taking our son?"

Brushing aside the frenzied people, they grabbed the young men hiding behind the protesting family members.

"Do as you are told, or there will be trouble," the soldiers shouted as they brandished their guns in the faces of the people. "You are conscripted into the army by order of the Republic of China. Our convoy will leave in one hour from the staging point by the post office. Your family may put your bedding roll and personal items into one bundle and bring it to you at the staging area."

Hustling the protesting young men into the waiting army vehicle and moving on to the next location to pick up more recruits was no easy task. At one home, fear filled the house as a young child ran and grabbed his father's leg shouting, "Papa, don't go! Papa, don't go!" The screaming child was roughly shoved aside by a burly soldier who was unmoved when the child rolled to the floor and hit his head on a cabinet.

"Don't take my husband," the young mother wailed. "What will become of me and my son?" But there was no answer as they shoved the man into the truck.

Angry mothers, running through the streets were crying in anguish, "They have kidnapped my son. Someone help us! Someone help us! Stop them from doing this!"

Frantically, family members gathered up bedding and personal effects, after recovering from the initial shock of losing a son or a husband. Rushing to the post office, they found scores of people in an uproar, demanding the release of their men. Only the ever-present movement of rifles aimed at them kept them at bay as they tried to storm the trucks.

Word spread like wild fire as frightened men sought to find a hiding place. The operation had been well planned with homes surrounded, cutting off all routes of escape. Some of the men fought back in one section of town, and would have succeeded in escaping if one of the solders had not fired his rifle in the air as a warn-ing to the people to submit or suffer the consequences.

"Next time we'll shoot to kill," they shouted. "Do as you're told, and stay away from these trucks."

They moved on to the next stop. Anching's younger brother rushed in from a neighbor's home where he had witnessed a brutal kidnapping. Shouting to Anching, he cried out, "Anching, hide somewhere quick! The soldiers are rounding up recruits, and I think they are headed this way."

The boy blurted out all he had witnessed as he urged Anching to flee. "The truck is coming," he shouted.

Mrs. Wen reacted immediately. "Quick," she ordered Anching. "Get under the bed and don't make a sound."

As he slid under the simple wooden frame, she pushed some bundles over him. He lay petrified, afraid even to breathe.

Hardly had Mrs. Wen finished arranging the bundles, when there came a pounding on the door that shook the whole house. "Hurry!" ordered a stern voice. "Open the door." The pounding continued as the impatient soldiers waited. "Open the door, or we will break it down," shouted the leader.

"I'm coming," called Mrs. Wen breathlessly as she managed to unbolt the door they had hurriedly locked a few moments before.

The soldiers pushed in rudely, and brushing Mrs. Wen aside, demanded, "Where is he? We know he's here. We've had the house surrounded all morning."

There were not many places to hide in this simple cottage. A curtain hung over an opening that served as a closet. The soldiers ripped it down and flung the cloth to the floor as they pulled cloth-ing off the rack in a mad search. "He's here somewhere. Better turn him over to us now," they warned. "Look under that bed," the officer commanded two of his men. They upended the bed uncer-emoniously and tossed it aside. The wooden frame hit the one window in the room and shattered the glass. Pulling the bundles of clothes and other things aside, they pounced on the trembling Anching cowering in a corner by the wall. Dragging him out, they shoved him toward the door with a rifle in his back.

"Oh, what are you doing to my son?" cried Mrs. Wen. "Let him go. He's only a teenager in high school. He's too young for the army. Please let him go."

"Shut up, and get his bedding roll ready. Bring it to the post office within the hour or he'll have nothing to keep him warm where we're going," he said cruelly as Anching was pushed into the back of the army truck.

"Fuching," called Anching as he was being shoved into the truck. "Run and tell Meiling what is happening." Fuching was the next youngest of the three sons of the Wen family. He took off like a shot for Meiling's home.

It was all over in a few minutes. The Wen home was in shambles. Mrs. Wen looked around frantically at the unbelievable destruction of the little they had. Realizing that there was not much time, she made some hasty decisions. "Suching," she ordered her youngest son, "run to the factory. Tell your father what has happened. Tell him they have taken Anching to the post office staging area. Hurry! Run as fast as you can!"

He was off like a streak of lightning. Quickly, the practical Mrs. Wen went to work preparing Anching's bedding roll and some personal effects. She grabbed his warmest clothing she had been preparing for the coming winter, and along with some other personal effects, she wrapped them in his bedding roll and tied them securely to prevent the loss of any of these precious possessions. Rushing to the post office, she hoped she would be in time. Mr. Wen arrived, breathless from the factory, angry at the cruelty of the army. Along with other men, they pushed their way toward the army officer in charge. "What are you doing to our sons?" they demanded. "This is against the law. You cannot kidnap these men like this!" they shouted.

"Stand back," he ordered. "I am simply obeying orders. Look, my men have rifles, and they will use them if necessary," he warned.

Fuching ran as fast as he could to Meiling's home. Reaching the doorway, he pulled the bell string insistently as he also pounded on the door. "Meiling! Quick. Open the door," he called. "I have an urgent message from Wen Anching. Hurry," he called. "There's no time to lose."

As he waited impatiently, he continued to pull the bell string vigorously, all the while shouting for someone to hurry and open the door.

Inside the house, Meiling heard the commotion. She dropped everything and ran as fast as she could to the door. Opening it a crack, she saw the distraught young boy. "What is it?" she asked anxiously.

"Meiling," he began as he tried to catch his breath. "Soldiers have taken Anching at gunpoint to the staging area by the post office. They are forcing him into the army and they are leaving within the hour. He told me to give you the message."

"What?" she screamed. "How can they do that?"

Mr. and Mrs. Woo came rushing to the door to see what the commotion was all about. Meiling had burst into tears. She flung herself into her father's arms, crying, "Father, do something. The soldiers are taking Anching into the army!" She sobbed uncontrollably as Fuching repeated the urgent message.

As Mr. Woo rushed out the door, he called back, "Quick! Meet me at the staging area. I'll go and see what I can do." His heart sank as he realized there was little he could do. Mrs. Woo took charge. "Meiling," she said in a soft yet commanding voice, "we must be very brave now. Get some things together for Anching just in case your father is unsuccessful in stopping the solders." In her heart she knew the answer. She had seen enough of Chinese soldiers. She knew it would be futile to resist.

With tears streaming down her cheeks, Meiling ran to her room. She paused a moment to think. "What will he need?" The first thing that came to her mind was a Bible. *He will need a Bible. I don't think his mother will think of that. And some paper and a pen. Oh, good. Here are a few stamps as well.* She looked around her room frantically. *What else can I give him?* A thought flashed through her mind. *Include your picture. He will be lonely. You don't know when you will see him again.*

Quickly she took a recent photo from an album and tucked it inside the Bible. *"Lord,"* she prayed, *"please watch over Anching no matter what happens. Help us to trust You at this time."*

"Run ahead," Mrs. Woo ordered. "You can get there quicker than I. I'll be there in a few minutes," she said as she gave Meiling a gentle push.

She didn't need any urging. She ran like a young deer, fast and sure-footed, as the tears flowed down her cheeks. Reaching the staging area, she saw the commotion and heard the shouting. Looking around wildly, she spotted Fuching with his mother. She had never met Mrs. Wen, but Fuching stepped in and said, "Mother, this is Meiling, Anching's classmate."

Mrs. Wen's eyes were red from crying. She quickly grasped Meiling's hands and sobbed, "This is awful. They have taken Anching. We are trying to get this bedding roll to him. I'm so glad you came. He has spoken of you so much."

"I've prepared this small package for him," Meiling answered, not taking time for any formal greetings. "Is there any way to include it with his bedding? He will need this Bible and the paper I have prepared."

"Oh, thank you," responded Mrs. Woo. "I never thought of those items. Yes, he will want a Bible I know. I'm so glad you remembered it. Here, let me push it inside this bundle," she said as she took the small package and began working it safely inside the bedding roll. "Now where is he being held?" she asked as she searched the trucks.

Mr. Woo had located the officer in charge, and with the other men, he was protesting these unlawful actions by the army. "You cannot do this," he said courageously. "It is against the law. Now let our men go," he ordered in a stern voice.

The other men recognized their honored high school principal, and they stepped aside to make room for him to approach the officer. "Your men were well taken care of in the high school for three days," he said as he recognized the officer. "You promised me that you would not harm our village and that you would repay us for the fuel your men used," he said boldly. "How can you take our young men like this? They are young fathers and students. Look, Anching is about ready to graduate. He is only a teenager. Please release him to us immediately."

The officer was stunned by the appearance of Mr. Woo. He could handle the protesting crowd, but the one who had given him sanctuary and provided so freely for the needs of the soldiers at the school was different.

"Mr. Woo, I'm sorry," he said sincerely. "I cannot stop what is happening. I am only a low-ranking officer obeying the commander. I know this is wrong, but I cannot prevent it," he ended lamely.

"Who is in charge?" demanded Mr. Woo. "I want to speak to him."

"I'm sorry, Mr. Woo," replied the officer, "he left already. The officer in charge is in the security car near the front, but no one will be allowed near him. Please be careful. The soldiers are ordered to maintain order even if they have to use their rifles."

"I must try anyway," replied Mr. Woo with a note of finality in his voice. He strode purposefully toward the head of the column with the other men close at his heels.

Meiling and Mrs. Wen and her children were searching frantically for Anching's vehicle. Each troop transport had six recruits crowded in with a dozen regular soldiers guarding them. Above the din of voices, Mrs. Wen heard the voice of her youngest son, Suching.

"Over here, Mother. Here's Anching over here."

Meiling rushed ahead to the truck with Fuching at her heels.

"Here he is," she cried out to Mrs. Wen.

Fuching pushed his way forward through the crowd with his mother right behind as relatives frantically attempted to get bedding rolls to their sons. The two brothers, Fuching and Suching, shoved Anching's bedding roll into the back of the truck. The soldiers on the outer edges reached out and pulled it in as Fuching shouted, "It's for Wen Anching."

Anching reached out and grabbed his bundle.

"Sit on it," a soldier ordered. "That's the only way it will be safe. Better learn that lesson right away," he said. "You're in the army now, and it can be rough," he advised.

Anching got his bedding stowed away under him when he heard Meiling's voice at the side of the truck. Looking out between the slats, he saw her. She never looked more beautiful with the tears on her cheeks. A huge lump rose in his throat. *When will I ever see her again,* he thought as he fought back the tears.

He reached out and took hold of her hand, "Meiling," he said, "be brave. The Lord will be with us. He will not forsake us now. That's what Pastor Yang preached on Sunday. Even though we cannot understand what is happening, the Lord will not forsake us. Remember, He is our Good Shepherd, and He knows our needs right now."

"I know," she replied as tears gushed from her eyes. "But why is it happening to us?" she cried. "Oh. Anching, when will I ever see you again?"

"I don't know," he replied solemnly, "but remember, I will never forget you, and I will spend the rest of my life looking for you. No matter what happens, I will come back and find you."

"I know, I know," she replied, "but suppose you are killed in the war? Then what? I cannot live without you," she sobbed.

"Yes, you can," he answered, "the Lord is our Helper and our Strength. Lean upon Him for the days ahead. And, if I don't make it back, I will meet you in heaven. Just never give up your faith in Jesus. You introduced me to Him. Now never forsake Him, and He will never forsake us."

"I packed my Bible in your bedding," she said. "And there's some writing paper and a pen in there, too. Write when you can."

"I will," he promised. "I will be thinking of you every day, and I will write as often as possible."

Mr. and Mrs. Wen pressed close to the side of the truck. "Son, I am so sorry I can do nothing to help you, but just as your God answered your prayer about my job, I believe He will help you now. And, son, I believe in Him. I will lead our family to the church. I promise," said his father who rarely said so many words. "Thank you for showing me the way," he said as the tears fell from his eyes.

"Oh, Father," Anching responded, "that means so much to me. I will never forget your words, and I will pray for you every day," he said as he gripped his father's hand.

Mr. Woo and some of the other men returned from the vain attempt to speak with the officer in charge. Seeing the Wen family and Meiling gathered at the side of the truck, he pushed his way through the crowd.

"Anching," Mr. Woo began as his voice cracked with emotion, "I've done the best I can to get you released, but I have failed." His shoulders shook with deep sobs as Mrs. Woo and Meiling clung to him.

As black billows of smoke poured out of the engine exhausts, people screamed for help, but there was none. Meiling grabbed Anching's extended hand. "Goodbye for now," she cried as the tears ran down her face. "God be with you. Meet me at the throne of prayer like pastor said. Be true, Anching. Be true to Jesus."

"I will," he answered. She was running faster now trying to keep up. There were too many people. She lost his grip.

"I will find you no matter where you may be," he shouted, "even if it takes the rest of my life."

"Oh, why did this happen to us?" sobbed Meiling as she clung to Mrs. Wen.

The older woman pulled her close as she too shook with sobs of pain and loss. "He brought us all so much joy in his newfound faith in God. For the first time in my life I could smile. Now, he's gone! I may never see him again."

Mr. Woo pressed close to his daughter, and taking her hand, he wept also. "This is the saddest day of my life," he choked through his tears. "I tried so hard. They deceived me. They stripped us of our food, and now they have taken our sons. Can the Communists be any worse?" he said with bitterness in his voice.

Chapter 4

TESTED TO THE LIMIT

A few of the new recruits cried silently while others cursed their bad luck. Anching sat silently with head bowed as the last glimpse of Meiling was etched on his mind forever. Once again he vowed he would find her again no matter where she would be, even if it took the rest of his life. He prayed silently for courage to face whatever lay ahead—loneliness, fear, and the possibility of death in battle. Pastor Yang's words flashed into his mind.

No matter where you go or whatever may be your circumstances, the Lord Jesus will be right there with you. He attempted to casually brush aside the tears in his eyes as he prayed lest someone see them and ridicule him, *Lord Jesus, help me now. If ever I needed You, it is now. Give me courage and strength to live for You in these circumstances and to exalt You at all times.*

The recruits were sandwiched in between the regular soldiers, each with a rifle cocked to prevent escape. The soldier next to him poked his side gently and whispered, "You must be a Christian. I overheard you talking to that beautiful girl, assuring her that if you did not come back, you would meet again in heaven."

"Yes, I am," he replied. "Are you?"

The soldier smiled as he nodded affirmatively. "Life will be better for both of us," he said. "I have been very lonely ever since I was forced into this army two months ago. You are the first Christian I have met."

One of the recruits overheard their subdued conversation. He spat on the floor and said derisively, "Okay, you Christians. Where is your God now? He didn't help us, did He? Don't pray for me when the battle starts! It won't help there either."

Anching quickly responded. "Don't blame God. He hasn't forsaken us. You'll see. We'll be praying for you every day. Count on it. By the way, what's your name?"

"Chu," grunted the surprised recruit. "But don't think you're going to convert me. I'm incorrigible, and I'll break your arm if you try."

"Back off, Chu," spoke up the Christian soldier. "When you need someone to pray for you, I bet you'll be the first to ask for help."

"Oh, yeah. Well, see if I ever come begging for any god to help me. I've made it through life this far without any help, and I'm sure I can make it the rest of the way."

"Well, just remember," said the Christian, "now there are two of us praying for you."

In spite of the sadness of the moment, everyone laughed as Chu scowled at the turn of events.

Suddenly the convoy ground to a halt amid a cloud of dust. "Toilet break," came the order down the line of trucks. "Just don't attempt to escape or we'll shoot," cautioned one of the guards of Anching's truck. The men did what they had to do, and then the recruits lined up at the back of the truck as the others lounged around smoking and talking. Suddenly, shouting erupted up front.

Shouts of "Halt" sounded from a truck ahead. "Halt, or I'll shoot." Several shots rang out. A recruit screamed as he slumped to the ground with blood gushing from several wounds. No one made any attempt to help him. They watched him writhe on the ground for a couple of minutes, and finally a soldier was ordered to check him out. "He's dead, sir," the soldier reported.

"Good shot," he commended his soldiers. Then in a loud voice, he shouted, "Let this be a lesson to you recruits and anyone else who may be thinking of escape. We tolerate no disobedience in this army. You obey, or you die," he said angrily.

The soldiers fidgeted uneasily with impatience. "What's holding up the works," someone shouted. "Let's get going."

A black limo overtook them and sped past with blaring horn.

"Hey, that's Pang's limo," shouted one of the conscripts. "I washed it every day. I'd know it anywhere. Bet the old man is paying them off for his son's release."

The word spread rapidly from truck to truck.

"Hey, Pang, what about us?" they shouted as they rose to scramble out of the trucks. Fortunately, no one was shot in the scuffle as the trucks lurched forward.

"Too bad we don't have rich fathers to bail us out," someone shouted.

"Bribery!" shouted another as the guards ordered them to be quiet.

A thousand thoughts flashed through Anching's head. *"Lord,"* he cried silently, *"the rich always seem to win."* He buried his face in his hands as his shoulders shook from inward sobs.

His newfound friend touched him gently and whispered, "Those who wait on the Lord renew their strength. They will mount up

75

with wings as eagles. You still have Jesus. He'll see you through. I know He's helping me."

"Yes, I really know that," he responded softly, "but it all seems so unfair. Luping is a rascal and he gets off because his father is rich. We try to follow God's Word, and we get taken."

"True, but what will the end be like for him?"

"Oh, forgive me. I know Luping's joys are temporary. Ours are eternal." Then, brightening with these thoughts he asked, "Say, what's your name? We never introduced ourselves. I'm Wen Anching."

"And I'm Chung Wenpei. Good to know you, Anching. I hope we can stay together for a long time. It will help a lot," he said with a smile.

The trucks rumbled on slowly day after day from town to town. Anching longed for his bed in his humble home in Puyang. He wondered about Meiling and how he would ever make contact with her again. He wondered, too, about his father who had said at their parting that he believed in Jesus and would lead his family to church. The thought cheered his heavy heart.

Lord, he prayed silently as the truck bounced along the rough road, *if this is what it takes to bring my father and family to You, then I rejoice in Your perfect ways, and I trust You to make it all right some day.*

They finally arrived at a staging area for recruits and immediately began the rigorous drills to prepare them for battle. A gruff army drill sergeant lined them up and read them the riot act. "You have one month to learn everything needed for battle. Learn fast or you'll be given extra duties to perform as punishment. And don't even think about running away," he shouted in their faces. "This building is patrolled by well-trained vicious dogs. No one has ever escaped. Do you understand?"

The weary recruits nodded their heads. He grabbed the nearest recruit by the chest and pulled him close to his face as he shouted again, "Do you understand? Answer, 'Yes sir, I do!'" The frightened man responded as demanded.

"And the rest of you. Do you understand?" They responded with a resounding, 'Yes sir, I do!'

The dreary days passed slowly for the lonely men. One very hot afternoon, after hours of marching and drilling with little rest and no water, Chu, weary from the long day, loudly cursed the sergeant to his face. Flushed with anger, the sergeant shouted heatedly, "I will teach you to show respect. Then see if you can stand and curse me!"

He ordered some regular guards nearby to hold him face down on the ground as he grabbed a bamboo pole. Everyone froze in place as Chu struggled with the guards.

"Hold him down," he shouted as he raised the pole above his head and whacked him soundly across the buttocks. Chu let out a blood-curdling scream as the bamboo pole struck him. He wriggled to free himself as the guards struggled to hold him down. Another blow crashed across his back, and another and another on his legs. Blow after blow rained down on the helpless man who squirmed less and less, and only groaned. Exhausted, the sergeant rested as he fumed at his recruits. "Don't ever disobey my orders or curse me like this stupid fool," he shouted hoarsely, "or you will suffer the same consequences." He threw down the pole as everyone stood speechless. One man vomited, and all felt weak and faint. He ordered them to stand there for the next twenty minutes and then he dismissed them to their barracks.

Chu lay groaning on the ground unable to get up. The rest of the recruits walked slowly back to the barracks, afraid to do anything to assist him. Once inside, Anching was the first to speak. "We must do something to help Chu," he said. "Who will help me bring him in?" He looked around at the frightened men. No one moved. "Then I will do it myself—somehow!" he said emphatically as he started toward the door.

"Wait, we'll help," responded two of the men. They joined him as the others watched apprehensively.

"We'd better use a blanket as a stretcher," Anching said as he picked up his blanket. "He will not be able to walk."

Looking in all directions, they saw no one in sight. Reaching Chu, still lying face down on the ground, they realized he had mercifully lapsed into unconsciousness.

"It will be easier to bring him in," Anching said. "One of you help me pick him up, and the other spread the blanket under him."

Lifting him as gently as possible, they struggled with his dead weight and laid him face down on his bunk.

"Bring some tea," Anching ordered as the men gathered around. He gently wiped the sweat and tears from Chu's face, and wet his lips with the warm tea. In a few moments, Chu stirred as Anching tried to spoon some tea into his parched mouth.

"He was stupid to curse the sergeant," said a recruit ruefully as he watched Anching.

"True," he replied, "but it was also a cruel thing to beat him so horribly. That is no way to treat a human being."

Anching sat by his side wiping his brow and wetting his lips with the tea. He stayed there all night, only catching a few winks of sleep himself as he ministered to the man. *Lord*, he prayed silently, *You know this is Chu, the man who said he didn't want anyone praying for him. You put me here to serve him. Now, let me show him Your love and transform his life.*

Toward morning, Chu fell into a fitful sleep, and that gave Anching a few hours of much-needed sleep. In the morning, he reported Chu's condition to the sergeant who ordered the medics to take him to the sick bay.

"May I have permission to visit him after drilling?" he asked respectfully as the sergeant looked at him suspiciously.

"Why do you make that request?" he asked. "Is he your friend?"

"No sir, I never met him until the day I was recruited in Puyang, and he hasn't been very friendly toward me because I am a Christian," he said boldly. "But I want to help him anyway because that's the way Christians live."

The sergeant looked at him for a long moment, and replied, "So, you're a Christian, are you? And do Christians help their enemies?"

"Yes sir," he answered astonished at his own boldness. "And we pray for them, too."

"What? You pray for your enemies? I never met a Christian before," he answered truthfully. "I'd like to see how this works," he said as he pulled a piece of paper from his pocket and scribbled permission to visit the sick bay once a day. "There," he said with a strange look on his face. "Only once a day," he said curtly as he walked away.

It was two weeks before Chu was able to hobble out of the sick bay and several more before he could move without pain.

"Why did you risk your life to help me?" he asked Anching one day. "I ridiculed you from the first day I met you. What's in this for you?"

Lord, help me, he prayed silently. "Chu," he began, "I have only done what Jesus would have done. He instructed us in the Bible to pray for our enemies or those who are unkind to us. I really haven't done anything very special. I just wanted to help you because you are my neighbor."

A long discussion followed as the man listened attentively to the story of the gospel.

"That's the first time I've ever heard anything about Christianity," he said bluntly. "I've been watching you ever since I first met you men. I must admit you really are different from the rest of us. You saved my life and helped me when I didn't deserve it. The other men told me you sat up with me all night the day I was beaten, and they said you were the one who came to my rescue out on the field. I want to thank you for putting yourself at risk for me when I was so unkind to you. I think I'd like to know more about this Jesus. Maybe He can help an incorrigible man like me!" Anching smiled as he answered, "Chu, He changed my life. He can change yours also."

Chapter 5

. . . .

THE COST OF WAR

Four months had passed since that fateful day when Anching disappeared down the road in a cloud of dust. Brokenhearted, Meiling could find solace nowhere except in her newfound faith and the church where she absorbed the teaching of Pastor Yang. With all hope shattered for a future with Anching, she plodded through the closing days of school and graduation.

Vainly she watched and waited for a letter, but each day ended as all the rest—in despair. With fall approaching, entrance into prestigious Wuhan University—that had been her goal for several years—lost its thrill, while a disheartening sense of hopelessness gradually took root in her heart. Only the words of the psalmist, "The steps of a good man are ordered by the Lord" bolstered her during those weary days.

The beautiful, clear weather of fall in the Yangtze River Basin was invigorating after the long, hot, sultry months of summer. The rice harvest was gathered in and harvest festivals were in full swing. Meiling thought back to the year before when Luping was chosen to represent their school in the speech contest as the result of his father's bribe. She had to guard her thoughts and pray for forgiveness whenever she thought of him. And now he too was graduating at the top of the class by the continued bribes of his father! Her frequent visits to the secluded spot by the river under the dragon spruce were times when she struggled with her anger and frustration, but each time it was prayer and meditation on the Word of God that refreshed her and gave her hope.

Returning from a time by the river, she saw her mother standing outside the gate of their home watching for her return. She was frantically waving an envelope. A letter from Anching?

*Tearing it open she read: My dear Meiling, life has been hectic since the day we rode away as captives of this army. Training has been rugged and sometimes cruel. The first month, I was virtually a cap*tive, confined to the barracks and under guard. Finally, with the basic training over, and being miles from home, we have been allowed some freedom. Finding a post office to mail this letter has been no easy task, and besides, the censors scrutinize every letter. I cannot tell you anything about where we are except to say we are at least 400 miles north of Puyang and expecting soon to engage the enemy. I have missed you so much and felt such times of despair, but the Lord has been my strength and put me with another Christian. Together, we have encouraged each other in the Word and at last, a man who claims to be incorrigible and who ridiculed me unmercifully, has joined us for Bible study. He was severely beaten with a bamboo pole for insolence. That gave me the opportunity to help him during the weeks of recovery, and it opened his heart to spiritual things. I am learning to trust God with each day, and even though they are long and dreary, I am discovering God's strength and help moment by moment. I hope you are also finding the Lord sufficient for each day's trials and disappointments. The future looks bleak as the whole country faces the horrors of war, but we can trust the One who died for us. As I promised when we parted, I will find you no matter where you are and no matter how long it takes. That is a promise. You may not hear from me often, or may not again because of the military situation, but I will never forget you, and I will *pray for you each day. In God's time, I truly believe He will bring us together again.*

She stopped reading aloud to her mother, and just threw her arms around her and wept tears of joy, "God is so good. He has answered my prayers and sent me this letter. I know He has not forsaken Anching or us. And, mother, I too, will wait and pray for that day to come."

Mrs. Woo looked at her daughter in amazement. "It could be years before you meet again. How can you be so certain that you will ever meet again?" she asked.

"I can't explain it, Mother, but I have the firm assurance in my heart that God will honor us and give us the desires of our hearts because we want to glorify Him above everything else."

She crushed the letter to her breast and found a quiet corner to read and reread its contents. It would be one of only two letters she would receive from him for many years to come, but it would be enough to sustain her and be a constant reminder that God is eternally faithful and He keeps His promises.

Oh, how she wanted to reply to this letter! There was no way to write to a soldier in the Chinese army in 1948. Instead, she would resort to prayer at God's throne where she and Anching had covenanted to pray daily for each other.

"Oh, Meiling," said Anching's mother the next day, "ever since I have been attending Pastor Yang's church, there has been such a wonderful peace in my heart even though this great sadness has come into my life. I am growing older and may never see my son again on earth, but I know I will meet him in heaven. And, imagine my husband attending the church!" she said with overflowing joy. "Now my whole family is attending the church and learning to walk with Jesus."

"That goes for my family, too," Meiling responded. "Only my father holds back from publicly declaring his faith because he is afraid of the consequences for our family when the Communists come."

As weeks became months, reports circulated that they would soon be deployed further north to engage the seemingly unstoppable enemy. Some soldiers spoke openly of their hatred for the Nationalist army because of the bad treatment they received. Some even went so far as to predict that the trenches they were digging would never be used. "This army will retreat rather than fight for the government that does not honor its promises!" they said over and over again in the barracks.

It was early December. The sharp north winds were beginning to blow and penetrate their thin garments, chilling everyone to the bone. On one of those particularly miserable days, orders were issued that early the next morning they would be starting north to the front lines. Weary men packed their gear and prepared for the worst. They would sponge off the poor people who hated and feared them. Up at the break of dawn, the soldiers formed a line by the trucks that would move them north. The road was not as dusty as it had been as the approaching winter had brought cold rain. They were warned that there might even be some snow in higher elevations. Having only thin garments, they wondered how they would survive.

"You know what you have to do," someone spoke up as they crawled into the truck. "Get some winter garments by any means you can from people along the way. It's the only way to survive," he said ruefully.

Traveling all day with little time to rest and stretch their legs, everyone looked forward to a place to sleep that night. The trucks pulled into a town that suddenly was emptied of people on the streets as they rushed to barricade their doors. Anching's truck was assigned with two others to a school for the blind where thirty-seven women were living. As they pounded on the court-yard gate, the men shouted impatiently, "Open up! This is the Nationalist army."

The woman in charge trembled as the pounding increased. *What could she do? How could she protect the blind women from these rough, undisciplined soldiers?* She ordered everyone to their rooms and instructed them to barricade their doors as much as possible. The pounding increased in intensity as the weary soldiers shook the courtyard gate and threatened to break it down. She made her way slowly to the gate in order to allow the frenzied women time to get their rooms barricaded.

"I'm coming," she shouted above the din. "Be patient. Every-thing is locked for the night."

As she lifted the last wooden pole from the slots that held the gate firmly shut, it was pushed opened and sixty men rushed un-ceremoniously into the courtyard. Many were shouting curses at the poor woman for being so slow as they unloaded their heavy packs and dropped them to the ground.

The lieutenant spoke authoritatively to the director and de-manded that they be allowed to stay for the night. "We will be leaving at the crack of dawn," he said, "and need a place to sleep tonight."

"But this is a school for blind women," protested the director. "There is no place here for your soldiers," she said as gently as possible. "Please, leave us alone, these are defenseless women."

"I have my orders," repeated the lieutenant. "We will stay here tonight," he said emphatically. "Now show us where we can sleep and cook our meal," he ordered sternly.

"There is a foreigner next door, a missionary who helps us. He must give permission. I cannot give it," she stammered as she stalled for time.

"My men are tired," the leader said impatiently, "and we must have space here. Get the foreigner immediately."

A staff member had already been dispatched to the house next door. The missionary picked up a prepared sign which stated that this school and dorm were under the protection of the Nationalist army. It was signed with the name of a high-ranking general. Rushing over, he found the soldiers impatiently milling around the inner court of the school grounds; it was obvious they were growing angrier by the minute.

"What's going on here?" he inquired in a loud voice that covered up his inward anxiety. He moved into the doorway of the building, blocking further entrance. "This is a dormitory for blind women and we cannot allow soldiers inside," he said forcefully. "Now please find some other place to spend the night. Look, here is the guarantee from General Fung that this school and these women are to be protected by the army."

Many voices were shouting louder now as they pressed closer to the missionary. He stood his ground in the middle of the doorway as the director and staff cowered behind him.

"Notice or no notice," the men shouted, "we're coming in." They shoved forward.

"Stand back," shouted the missionary. "Read the general's orders. You cannot come in here."

At that, a brash soldier cocked his rifle, and shoved it in his chest. "Move over," he shouted above the din of voices clamoring to get in, "or I will shoot you!"

With the rifle pressed against his chest, the missionary's knees felt like rubber. *What to do now?* Suddenly, out of the darkness, a hand reached out, and pulled the soldier back, ordering him to put his rifle down. The leader spoke more softly, "Sir, I promise that my men will not molest the women. If you allow us to enter the building, we will occupy only the ground floor. We'll cook out here in the courtyard and we'll not use any of your fuel. Just let my men in. You can see that they are very impatient and angry. I cannot guarantee anything if you refuse."

The missionary had regained his composure, and recognizing the futility of further resistance as well as the danger of the situation, he replied, "Lieutenant, if you promise not to harm the women nor use our supplies, you may enter this general area on the ground floor. But, please order your men to be kind to these poor, frightened women."

"Good," replied the leader with relief. "My men will not molest anyone." He turned and spoke to his men and explained the circumstances. "Agreed?" he asked his men in a loud voice.

"Yes, agreed," they shouted back. The missionary stepped aside as the men pushed in to find a spot to unroll their bedding.

The staff people gathered around the missionary at the far end of the large ground floor room. "Will they keep their word?" they asked anxiously.

"I believe they will," he said. "The lieutenant seems to be a reasonable man, and besides, we will pray and ask the Lord to surround each one with His protecting presence. Let's do that right now." He quietly led the women in a prayer for protection. As he closed the prayer, they all echoed a strong "Amen."

"Oh, thank you, pastor," the director responded. "I believe the Lord will protect us tonight."

As they looked up, there were three men standing nearby smiling. "My name is Wen Anching," one of the men said, "and these are my friends, Chung Wenpei and Chu Wantai. We are all believers. Our big friend here, Chu, is as strong as an ox. He is a new believer of just a few days. We have joined you in prayer, and we will make sure that these men keep their promise. No one will be hurt tonight!"

"Oh, praise the Lord," murmured the women. "God has sent you as angels to watch over us. O, thank You, Jesus."

"No, we are not angels," Anching replied. "We are just men who have been saved by God's grace. We too are on our way to heaven," he said with an infectious smile. "We will be on guard here all night, so don't worry. Our lieutenant is a good man, and he will keep his word."

The three men took up their position by the stairway to make certain no one went upstairs. With their evening meal over, the weary men soon settled down to sleep. There were no further incidents, and the blind women slept soundly, knowing that these Christian soldiers were sent by God to protect them. As the soldiers slept, Anching hurriedly wrote a letter to Meiling. In the morning, the director found the three men eating their breakfast right at the foot of the stairs.

"How can I thank you for what you have done for us?" she asked warmly. "You have been God's messengers to us. Thank you, and God bless you."

Anching held out the letters that he and Wenpei had written. "Would it be possible for you to mail these letters to our families?" he asked. "Here is some postage money. We cannot leave our group to find a post office," he said, "but we would appreciate it very much if you would do this for us."

Taking the letters, she said, "Please, it would be our special privilege to mail these for you. Keep the money. I know you don't have very much. This will be our gift of thanksgiving to God for your help in protecting us. And we will pray that you will be protected in battle."

"Please pray that we will be able to live lives pleasing to God before our fellow soldiers," Wenpei responded. "I was alone until Anching joined me several months ago, and now we have a new brother in our circle. We hope many more will come and join us."

As the men began loading up the trucks again, the director and staff brought some fresh steamed bread from the kitchen and passed them out to the troops. "This is a gift in Jesus' name," they said as the men gratefully received this unexpected gift. "God be with you and protect you," they called to the men. For the three believers, they presented some oranges as a special gift of appreciation.

"Praise the Lord," they kept repeating. "We will never forget you and your kindness to us."

The other soldiers looked on, quietly observing all that the director said to the three Christians. That was enough to keep them talking for hours.

One man spoke up and said, "You Christians are different from the rest of us. Your circumstances are as bad as ours, yet you were kind to those women. There must be some special secret you know that we don't," he said. "In fact, I would like to know more about this Jesus you speak of."

The three men beamed with joy. *Praise the Lord,* they thought. *Our prayer is already being answered.* "All of you are welcome to join us as we read and study the Bible," they answered. "You will never be disappointed with Jesus," they assured the men. Looking at Chu, the others wondered what kind of a miracle had happened to this rough man who nodded his approval. As the troops drove on, the men in Anching's truck asked many questions about Christianity. Wenpei and Chu shared in the testimony time, but it was Anching who took the lead. He was as natural at sharing his faith as eating his food. There probably has never been another truckload of soldiers who listened more attentively.

The cannons were booming in the distance as the trucks reached their destination near the front. The smell of smoke and death seemed to hang in the air, leaving everyone with a deep sense of loneliness and fear. Jumping out of their truck, the troops soon located the weathered tent they were assigned to.

"Not much to keep us warm," some grumbled. "These thin summer outfits won't provide much protection from the wind. And they expect us to fight like this?"

At least there was a good supply of wood that was quickly used to start a fire and cook their rice. Standing around the warm fire with a cup of hot tea in hand, their spirits revived as they waited for their rice to cook. In a few minutes they ate ravenously and swallowed several more cups of tea.

"We'll be deployed to the front in two days," the sergeant informed them. "Better get as much rest as you can before then. When we hit the fighting line, there won't be any more comforts like this warm fire and food."

Every man ate his fill of the hot food in silence, each contemplating the dangers and sacrifices that lay ahead. The three Christians huddled in a tight circle before turning in for the night, praying for the men who would soon face death.

On the third day, a convoy of ten trucks started toward the front about twenty miles away. Reports of the bitter fighting were trickling in with the wounded. Only one very tired medic was there to care for the wounded. Some soldiers were pressed into service to move the wounded to the medical tent and then on to one that served as a dispensary. Conditions were intolerable, and the cold was bitter. Many were in shock with frozen blood-soaked garments, making it doubly difficult to care for them.

The convoy started out in the eerie pre-dawn darkness, and slowly crept along without lights lest they become a target for the enemy. They had to pass through a narrow section of road bounded on either side by thick underbrush and trees. It was the perfect spot for an ambush and all approached it with dread.

Suddenly, the stillness of the morning was shattered as machine guns rattled on either side of the road. The men hit the floor of the trucks as bullets sprayed them from front to back. A powerful blast from a bomb destroyed the two lead trucks. Pandemonium broke loose in the darkness. The wounded never had a chance to escape the burning trucks. Screaming with pain, they cried in vain for help, but the flames engulfed them and silenced their voices forever. The third driver jammed on his brakes at the instant of the blast, but not before plowing into the burning truck ahead. Jumping out of their truck, they barely escaped the inferno. The noise of shouting and shooting filled the night air as confusion reigned everywhere among the untested troops. Adrenaline surged through their veins as they fired back into the darkness. Suddenly, a grenade thrown from the bushes came tumbling toward the group of men. Everyone scrambled for safety except one alert soldier who picked it up and lobbed it back into the bushes. Seconds later it exploded, wiping out the machine gun nest that had pinned them down. The screams of the wounded and dying in the darkness sent shivers up everyone's spine as machine guns rattled on either side of the road.

The dead and wounded were loaded into the last truck and returned to camp while the first three trucks of the convoy were consumed in the fiery blaze. Three hours passed before the wreckage was cleared away and the convoy started forward again. By eight o'clock they arrived at the forward position where a chow line had been set up for the hungry soldiers.

The sergeant commended his soldiers for their prompt response to the ambush. "Looks like we lost twelve men and sixteen wounded," he reported. "We were lucky that Tang was swift enough to lob that grenade back into the machine gun nest or none of us would be here," he said with a nod toward Tang. "We owe you our lives today. Now men, be on your guard. Do what you need to do to protect one another, and fight like devils or all will be lost."

The men walked up to the front lines where other soldiers were busy digging deep trenches.

"Grab a shovel and go to work," they were ordered. "This is our next line of defense," a lieutenant called out. "Dig them deep enough to protect yourself and make them as comfortable as possible. You're going to be here for a while."

Keeping warm was a major concern of all the men in the trenches, but it also provided opportunity for discussions about the meaning of life and death. Anching was kept busy answering those questions, but occasionally, he felt the sting of ridicule.

"It is better to obey God and suffer persecution than to receive the praise of people who know nothing of the joys of eternal life," Anching said to his two friends one day when several men were merciless in their ridicule. "My pastor back home often referred to Moses who chose to follow God and suffer persecution rather than enjoy the pleasures of sin for a few moments of ease."

"That's right," replied Wenpei soberly. "And the ridicule some have heaped on us is nothing compared to the suffering Jesus endured or what many Christians are suffering in the areas occupied by the Communists."

Chu listened attentively to these discussions, and like a sponge, he absorbed everything and applied it to his life. "There is nothing in all the world that would persuade me to return to my old life," he said emphatically.

"Praise God you feel that way, Chu," replied Anching. "But remember, we are all weak human beings who do not know what we will do under extreme pressure. Remember, it was Peter who told the Lord he would never forsake Him, but he did."

"I didn't know that," Chu confessed. "Tell me about it."

For the next hour or so, the three men discussed Peter's denial. Chu was moved by the story of Peter, and in the dim light of their little fire, the others saw this rough man wipe the tears from his eyes. "No matter what happens," he said, "I want to be a true witness for Jesus at all times."

"I think they're getting ready for an assault on our position," the sergeant said after several hours of constant bombardment. "We've got to hold this pass at all costs," the captain told me. "If they break through here, they will overrun our command post."

He had hardly finished speaking when the scream of a shell seemed to be coming in extremely low. Everyone sought whatever protection he could find in the trench and waited fearfully for the impact. It landed with a horrific blast about 100 yards from Anching and his friends. The screams of the wounded men filled the morning air as rescuers rushed to help them. In the eerie light of dawn, it was obvious that two of the men were dead. Three were wounded; one appeared to be in serious condition. They did what they could to stop the bleeding, and then rushed them to the command post a half-mile back.

The fight continued for another half-hour. "They want this pass," the sergeant said, "and I expect there'll be an attack soon.

Make sure you all have enough ammunition, and keep a sharp look out."

The third day of constant bombardment started as usual.

"This is it," someone shouted. "Here they come," echoed through the trenches.

The machine gunners temporarily turned the enemy back. Adrenaline was surging through the bodies of men on both sides of the pass. Tingling with fear and excitement, they watched intently and fired at everything that moved. With both armies intent on winning the battle, the fighting was fierce and desperate. Anching's group had only been together for a few months, but for green troops never before in battle, they fought remarkably well under such intense fire. A burst of fire erupted several hundred yards in front of them as the enemy attempted a frontal assault. Their own machine gunner responded instantly, sweeping the area with a withering barrage of gunfire. The screams of the wounded soon turned to silence as the enemy retreated.

"They'll be regrouping for another attack," shouted the sergeant. "Reload your weapons and get ready," he commanded.

"I remember the first time I met you, Anching," said Chu as he wiped the perspiration from his forehead even though the morning was cold. "I ridiculed you and joked about you praying for us in battle. I'm glad you prayed for me before the battle, and now I am a believer and ready to die and stand before my God. You other guys, remember what Anching has been telling us about Jesus? Better confess your sin while you can and be ready to stand before a holy God."

The conversation was cut short as the battle started up again with more shells falling close by. Ground troops were attempting to scale the high ground overlooking the pass. The noise of battle was deafening as bombs burst and machine guns rattled from both sides. Without warning, an airborne grenade landed in the trench. Men scrambled to find protection. Instinctively, Chu ran forward, picked it up to toss it back, but it exploded with a sickening blast. His body was hurled backward and fell to the ground in a twisted, bloody heap. Unhurt, Anching picked himself up and leaped forward to help his friend Chu. He cradled the dying man in his arms as another soldier attempted to stop the bleeding.

"Chu," he cried, "can you hear me? You saved our lives."

"An . . . ching," he gasped with difficulty. "They're . . . coming."

"Who's coming?" he asked as he bent low to catch every word.

"Angels," he breathed heavily. "They're . . . singing. It's . . . it's beautiful. It's . . . so bright. Anching . . . they're . . . calling . . . my name." His voice was just a whisper as his lifeblood oozed from his body. "Thank . . . you . . . for showing . . . me . . . the way."

Suddenly, Chu opened his eyes wide, and struggling upward, he lifted his uninjured arm toward heaven. "I'm coming, Lord," he said clearly as Wenpei rushed over.

"All heaven is rejoicing," Anching said to him. "The angels have come to take him home. Oh, thank You, Jesus for saving Chu, and giving him eternal life. Chu," he spoke tenderly to his dying friend, "Wenpei is here also. We'll see you again some day in heaven."

"Yes," he spoke with much greater difficulty, "I'll . . . be . . . waiting. Jesus . . . I'm coming . . . home," he gasped.

A smile spread over his bloodied face as he breathed his last and lay in Anching's arms.

"What was that all about?," asked a soldier nearby. "I didn't see any angels or hear any singing."

Anching gently laid his friend down on the ground, and said to the soldier, "No, we couldn't see the angels who came to take Chu home to heaven, and we couldn't hear the singing as he entered the gates of heaven, but it was very real. Jesus came to welcome home a sinner who trusted Him for salvation."

Everything had grown quiet as the enemy retreated after suffering severe casualties. They were unable to mount another attack for two weeks. Anching and Wenpei were given permission to carry their dead friend back to the main camp, and there they buried him in a simple grave. The two men knelt by the grave and softly sang *Amazing grace how sweet the sound, that saved a wretch like me, I once was lost, but now am found; was blind, but now I see.*

After prayer, they rose and walked quietly back to their tent. Searching around, they found some wooden slats and fashioned a crude cross on which they wrote in Chinese, Chu's name and the words, *T'a ai Yesu,* meaning, *He loved Jesus.*

"We will meet again in heaven, dear brother," Anching said softly as he pushed the cross into the ground.

In the days that followed, all of the men in the unit went out to the simple grave and read the words on the cross. "He really became a different man after he met you two Christians," they all remarked.

Chapter 6

. . . .

THE ARMY COLLAPSES

The night had been long and miserable. Strong winds swept through the trenches as the men tried to get some sleep and stay warm. With temperatures near the freezing point, both were impossible. Weary from the long ordeal, the government troops were unprepared for the heavy barrage of artillery that relentlessly pounded their positions. Anching's unit braced for the worst as they waited in the darkness for the inevitable assault. Peering intently out into the darkness, tension began building, for somehow they knew that this was the morning for an all-out assault.

An unearthly silence descended on the battlefront as the artillery fell silent and the men listened for any sound of the enemy. Suddenly, the silence was broken with the piercing screams of the enemy as they lunged forward, guns blazing. In a few seconds the din of battle grew loud and intense.

"We can hold our position," shouted the sergeant to his men as wave after wave of enemy soldiers tried unsuccessfully to take the high position. "They're pulling back again," he shouted in encouragement to his men. "Good work," he called as he took account of his men. "None wounded or killed. They can't take us with a frontal assault," he called out. "I hope the men on our flanks have been as successful as we have been."

The lull in battle gave Anching and Wenpei opportunity to exchange a few words.

"How are you doing?" Anching asked as he looked over at his friend. It was still an hour to sunrise, but light enough to see the worried look on his face. "Not hurt are you?"

"No, I'm okay," he replied shakily, "but I have an uneasy feeling in my heart; sort of a foreboding feeling of heaviness, as if something is going to happen to one of us."

"I know what you mean," Anching replied, "but remember, death is only a gateway to heaven."

"I know," he replied, "but ever since Chu was killed, I have this feeling that we will soon be parted. You have encouraged and helped me so much. If anything happens to you, I will suffer a great loss," he said honestly.

"Your friendship has helped me also. I don't want to think of separation, even for a short while. I feel the loss of Chu every day, but he wouldn't want to come back to this miserable existence if he had a choice. He's looking on the face of Jesus right now, and he's really smiling."

Waiting for the inevitable in the semi-darkness, the two friends joined hands, and with their eyes wide open, searching the area in front of them, they prayed for each other.

"If anything happens to me," Anching said when they had finished, "please try and get a message through to Meiling. I will do the same for your parents. And, then whoever goes first, wait at the gate of heaven for a grand reunion."

Unexpectedly, the noise of battle erupted on their right flank as guns blazed and heavy shells rained down on the troops again. Then, off to the left, the rapid fire of machine guns indicated the enemy was attempting to break through on both their flanks.

"Pull back," shouted the sergeant above the roar of battle. "The enemy has broken through on our right about two miles above us. We'll have to abandon this position or be trapped. Our troops are in retreat. Fight like men," he shouted, "and hold them off as long as possible. That will give our troops a chance to escape."

They pulled back a half-mile and set up on a high rise that gave them a commanding position, but none too soon. As the sun broke over the horizon, the enemy was pouring through the pass they had protected so long with guns blazing on two sides. The battle raged for two hours with many casualties on both sides. Anching's unit was preparing for another withdrawal when Wenpei screamed in pain as bullets pierced his left shoulder.

"Go," shouted Wenpei. "I can't make it. I'll meet you in heaven someday. Be faithful to the end and serve Jesus with all your heart."

"I won't leave without you," Anching shouted back. "Here, let me help you," he said as he put Wenpei's right arm over his shoulder. "Hold on if you can," he implored as he half-carried, half-dragged his friend as the army retreated. And then, Anching saw it. A small opening to a cave hidden in the deep foliage. The shouts of the victorious troops rushing forward meant there were only a few minutes before they would be overtaken. He pulled Wenpei toward the cave entrance as his friend groaned in pain. Hardly had they entered the cave, when enemy soldiers ran by in hot pursuit of the retreating army.

"We're safe for the moment," he whispered. "I don't think anyone will stop to look in here. How's your shoulder?" he asked as he pulled back his shirt to take a look. "Oh, that's an ugly wound all right, but if we can stop the bleeding, I think you'll be okay."

"You shouldn't have stayed behind like this," Wenpei said reproachfully. "Now you're behind enemy lines, and that means it will be very dangerous for you."

"I would never forsake you, my friend," Anching said firmly. "The Lord opened up this cave for us at just the right moment, didn't He? And, I believe that He will see us through. Now try and rest. You'll need all your strength in these next few days if you are to make it."

The sound of battle receded in the distance as Anching crept to the entrance of the cave to look out and listen. *Lord,* he prayed silently, *what shall I do? You provided this cave for us, and we are safe for the moment. But what next?*

The words of Psalm 91:1 flashed into his mind. "Thank You, dear Lord," he spoke out loud. "Yes, that's it. 'He who dwells in the shelter of the Almighty, will rest in the shadow of the Almighty. I will say of the Lord, He is my refuge and my fortress, my God, in whom I trust.'" *Oh, precious Jesus, thank You for the promise of Your protection and help. I don't know what we'll do, but we will wait for Your directions and help.*

He crept back to Wenpei who had fallen into a fitful sleep. Weary from the long night and the excitement of the battle, Anching lay down and was soon fast asleep. It was dusk when he awoke. Wenpei slept on. *That's God's provision for him,* he thought, and feeling his water canteen still on his belt, he thought, *and He even protected my water! How good the Lord is.* Wenpei's canteen had taken a shot that deflected the bullet from his kidneys and spared his life. *Amazing,* he thought. *That canteen spared his life!*

Wenpei's eyes fluttered open. He looked around at the strange surroundings in the semi-darkness of the cave. "Where are we?" he asked in a dazed voice.

"We're in a cave behind enemy lines. The battle flowed past us and we're safe for the moment."

"Oh, my shoulder," he groaned. "Am I really still here?" he asked disappointedly. "I expected to wake up in heaven."

"Not yet," laughed Anching as he took off his undershirt and tore it into strips to make a sling for Wenpei. "Here, this will keep you from moving your arm and starting the bleeding again. Now have a little drink. We have this one canteen between us. You'll need it," he said as he helped him take a drink. Anching longed for a sip as well, but he knew his friend would need it more. The night wore on, and in the restful silence of the forest, they both got a little much-needed sleep.

Both were unaware of the tragedy of the battle. The Communists had completely overwhelmed the government troops, and many had died. Those who survived were in full retreat and running as fast as they could to escape death at the hands of the victors. Word of the defeat reached General Chiang Kai-shek, president of China and general of the army. He knew it was all over, and time to escape to Taiwan where he would set up his government and plan to retake the mainland once again. His plane lifted off that evening, carrying the general and his aides.

His troops scattered, seeking only to save their own lives. They commandeered every truck or vehicle they could find. The trains heading south were jammed with weary men, and many wounded. Even the tops of the train cars were packed with fleeing refugees. Many hung on the sides, but during the cold of the night, they lost their grip and fell off to die along the tracks. Every man sought to get rid of his uniform and blend in with the public now fleeing in panic as well. The roads were littered with the dead. Many infants and little children were abandoned in the melee of defeat, too young to travel.

China's long night had just begun. Millions would die in the two decades to come, and many Christians would endure unheard-of torture for their faith. It seemed that the enemy of the souls of men had finally succeeded. The light was going out all over China. What the enemy of mankind did not count on, however, was the eternal presence of the Holy Spirit who dwelt in the relatively few believers in the country. In the months and years ahead, the Communists would succeed in driving out all missionaries, and would succeed in crushing the church through persecution and death. People in the west would wonder for years what was happening behind the bamboo curtain. They could only pray that God would intervene and bless His faithful people. Meanwhile, back in the cave, a miracle was about to happen.

The sun was beginning to peek through the trees of the forest as Anching looked out from the safety of the cave. Could it be that less than twenty-four hours had passed since his unit pulled back in defeat? As he cautiously looked out of the cave, he wondered what he should do. Wenpei needed medical attention. They had not eaten since before the battle, and with every drop of water saved for Wenpei, Anching knew their situation was desperate. Suddenly, he heard the sound of footsteps approaching. Fear clutched at his heart as he moved back into the shadows of the cave and waited anxiously. Through the small opening he saw two men—civilians, pause by the cave's entrance. His heart was pounding as he lifted his voice silently to the Lord in prayer for help and guidance.

"Ah, what a terrible battle that was yesterday," one man said to the other. "There are many dead all over this area. What shall we do?"

"First, we must see if there are any still living, and then do what we can to help them."

"It will be very dangerous for us to be caught up here. Suppose the Communists return?"

"What would Jesus do?" asked the first man who was the local pastor. "Would He not stop and help the wounded no matter what the cost would be to Him personally? Remember the story of the Samaritan who stopped to assist the man who was beaten and left along the road for dead? We will do the same. We will help whomever we find, government or Communists troops."

Anching could hardly believe his ears. Christians were just a few feet from him. A miracle was happening right before his eyes. He crept forward silently to hear better. As the men rested, the pastor spoke. "I feel that God has sent us up here this morning to help someone. Let's pray that He will direct us to the needy."

With that he began to pray earnestly that God would guide them to any wounded men in the area. Finishing his prayer, both men joined in saying a strong "Amen."

From just inside the cave's entrance another "Amen" sounded forth. The two men jumped to their feet, startled by the voice from the cave.

"Who's there?" called the pastor.

Anching moved out into the bright sunlight of the morning. "Oh, brothers," he spoke with emotion, "God has sent you to help us. I am a believer and I have been praying for God to work a miracle. My friend is in the cave and he is wounded. He needs help badly."

"Oh, praise the Lord," the pastor responded with joy as he took hold of Anching's hand. "God has led us to you and your friend."

Leading the two men into the cave, Anching said, "I am Anching and this is my brother in the Lord, Wenpei. He was wounded in the battle yesterday, and we just barely escaped into this cave as the Communist troops rolled by. God has spared our lives. Oh, pastor, can you help my brother?"

"Yes, yes, of course we can." Addressing Wenpei he asked, "Can you walk my brother?"

"I don't think I can," Wenpei groaned. "I am too weak."

To his companion he said, "Lead Anching back to my house, and then bring a couple of strong men back with a stretcher. I will stay here with Wenpei." Turning to Anching he said, "You will be safe with us temporarily. The Communists troops have rushed on and none are around just now. We'll trust the Lord to help us to know what to do next. We will walk by faith, step by step," he said comfortingly.

"I will be waiting for you, Wenpei. Just take it easy. God has sent His angels to help us," he said as a big smile spread over his handsome face.

The missionary at the blind school addressed the frightened women gathered in the little meeting room. "We will prepare to leave in the morning. The Communist troops are continuing to push south," he said sadly. "I must get you all to Taiwan and safety. To remain here will be too dangerous, and from all reports, handicapped people are treated very badly, especially the women. Each one will be permitted only what you can carry yourself. Be prepared for a difficult journey, but remember, the Lord is going before us to prepare the way. We will take the train to Wuhan, and from there, I hope we can get a river steamer to Shanghai, and then on to Taiwan."

Following prayer, the women dispersed to their rooms to prepare for the long journey. Early the next morning, they started out to the train station with six or seven blind women walking behind a teacher, each with one hand on the shoulder of the woman before them. They trudged confidently in step through the street to the train station as neighbors came out to bid them a sad farewell. The missionary had been able to secure second-class seats for the entire group, and although it was much more costly, it was the only safe way for the women to travel on to Wuhan.

Twenty-four weary hours later, the party of thirty-seven blind women and eight teachers pulled into the train station in Hankou, and then continued on across the Yangtze River to Wuhang. What a time of rejoicing they all had as Pastor Yang and several of the Christians welcomed them and made them comfortable in the strange surroundings.

"Praise the Lord, you all arrived safely," said Pastor Yang as he welcomed his long-time missionary friend. "I got your telegraph message, and a friend in the steamship company has already reserved places for your entire group to Shanghai. You should be there in about four days."

"Oh, praise the Lord!" replied the missionary. "How good the Lord has been to us in the midst of this terrible ordeal."

Later that evening the missionary shared with his pastor friend the events of the night the government troops entered the home of the blind women.

"God sent us some angels to help us that night," continued the missionary. "Angels?" inquired the pastor. "How was that?"

"Well, it's an amazing story. The director called me over to try and keep the troops out of the building, but I soon discovered that I was quite helpless. It was really frightening when a soldier pushed his rifle right into my chest and ordered me to move over or be shot. It was a terrifying moment, I can assure you."

"That really must have been," responded Pastor Yang. "Then what happened? I know you didn't get shot, so the Lord must have protected you in some miraculous way."

"Yes, He did. Just at that moment, an officer's hand appeared out of the darkness, and pulled the soldier out of the way, and ordered him to put down his gun. But that wasn't all. After I negotiated with the captain for his troops to occupy only the ground floor, I prayed with the director and staff. As we all said, 'Amen,' there were three soldiers standing with us, and they also echoed an 'Amen.'"

"They did?" responded the pastor in surprise. "There aren't many Christians in the army!"

"One man introduced himself and said he was from a suburb of Wuchang called Puyang, and his name was Wen Anching."

"Wen Anching!" exclaimed the pastor excitedly. "We know him. He's from this church!

"You know him?' asked the surprised missionary. "Then maybe you know Woo Meiling."

"Of course, we do," spoke up Mrs. Yang excitedly. "She attends this church regularly."

"Well, that's another miracle," exclaimed the missionary. "Anching asked me to send this letter to Meiling, but because the situation deteriorated so rapidly and we had to flee, I decided it would be safer to hand deliver it. I must meet Meiling as soon as possible."

"I will see that you do in the morning, but tell me the rest of the story about Anching."

"I will," he replied. "That young man and his friends said they would camp at the foot of the stairs and prevent any of the soldiers from molesting the women. They had a big, strong man by the name of Chu with them. I think he could have cleaned up on the whole troop if they had tried to go upstairs. Those three men were God's angels sent to protect the women that night."

"And what else can you tell me about Anching," asked the pastor solemnly. "Have you had any further word from him?"

"Not one word, but I know there was a big battle going on north of us. The news filtered down that the government troops were not holding up too well and if you wanted to escape, it was best to go immediately. That's when I decided we must take these women to Taiwan."

"You are doing the right thing. Word reached us that women in a deaf school were brutally raped and beaten when the Communists rolled into the town. When they found out they were Christians, they beat them unmercifully in an attempt to get them to renounce their faith in Jesus. But not one yielded under that awful pressure. Every one of them died singing as best they could, the praises of the Lord."

"That's why I must get these women to Taiwan as soon as possible," replied the missionary. "Please pray that we will not be trapped anywhere along the way. I cannot bear to think of the suffering these women would endure."

"These next years are going to be very difficult for Christians especially. Many will be called upon to suffer, and even make the supreme sacrifice of our lives, but we will not give up," added Pastor Yang.

Meiling dabbed at the tears that wouldn't stop coming as the missionary recounted the story of Anching's heroism.

"He is truly a remarkable young man," the missionary said, "and very brave also."

"You must visit his mother and father today," Meiling replied. "They will be overjoyed with this news."

The stretcher-bearers arrived at the pastor's home later in the afternoon where a believer who worked at the local hospital cleaned up the ugly wound.

"If we can keep infection from setting in," she said, "maybe you could be able to travel in about a week."

"It is best if we keep the presence of these men a secret," the pastor instructed. "Anyone wanting to curry favor with the Communists will report us and cause us great harm. Now we must pray that Wenpei's wound will heal quickly and that God will protect them along the way."

"Pastor," Anching spoke, "you have already risked your lives to help us. We must move on in the morning. To stay here in your home will only cause you great pain and suffering. Can you find us an old cart? Wenpei can hide under vegetables or something, and I will pull the cart like a farmer. We may be able to escape that way."

Wenpei raised his head, and looking at his friend with steady, piercing eyes, he said earnestly. "Anching, you can't risk your life again for me. Go on; escape while there's time. I will probably die from infection anyway."

Anching knelt immediately by his side, and taking his hand in his said emphatically, "Wenpei, I will never forsake you, nor will I ever leave you behind. We are brothers in Christ. When I needed help, you were there to help me. I cannot leave you and save myself."

Moved to tears by the devotion of these two men, the pastor spoke quietly, "Brothers," he said, "Anching is right. There is not much time, but it will be too soon to leave tomorrow. Maybe a day or two will be needed for Wenpei to be strong enough to travel. Anching, I like your plan. A farmer pulling a cart will not make anyone suspicious, and with the Lord's help, you should be able to slip through the lines and escape further south. I recommend that you try to reach the British Colony of Hong Kong. The Communists will certainly hunt down every former government soldier and execute them."

"I can find a cart that will be long enough for Wenpei to lie on," spoke up one of the men, "but I don't think vegetables will be good for the load. They would spoil within a few days. I think hay would be better."

"You are right, Brother Li," the pastor said. "Let's get started preparing what our brothers will need for their journey. In the meantime, you ladies prepare them some nourishing food, and then let them get some sleep. They must be strong for the journey ahead of them."

Two days later a cart was ready with a frame that would keep the hay off Wenpei.

"I still think this is too dangerous for you, Anching," he pleaded. "Go on without me. When I am stronger I will follow."

"Please do not mention this again, Wenpei. I will not leave you. We will escape together, and trust the Lord to guide our steps. If it is His will, we will reach Hong Kong, but if not, we will die together."

After the evening meal, the Christians gathered together in the pastor's home. They sang praises to the Lord, and committed the young men into His care.

"I think it best that you leave by three o'clock to avoid being seen by townspeople. Unbelievers will be tested in the days ahead and they will report us to save their necks. Let's hope and pray that no one discovers you men," the pastor said solemnly.

After a heart-moving prayer by the pastor, the believers said good-bye to their young friends. "God be with you," they repeated as each grasped their hands. "We shall meet again some day in the presence of Jesus. Be faithful to the end."

By two-thirty, Wenpei was gently laid on the cart and the frame placed over him. As Anching watched, the hay was loaded on.

Dressed as a farmer with straw hat and sandals, he looked authentic. He stepped between the poles of the cart, adjusted the strap to his shoulder, and slowly started down the road to Hong Kong some five hundred miles away. The Christians had prepared food to last them several days and pressed money into Anching's hand as they bid them good-bye. Slowly and quietly, the cart moved through the sleeping town, as the two men began their trip south.

Chapter 7

THE ORDEAL

The pastor and the small band of believers watched silently as the cart slowly moved out of sight. "Oh, our heavenly Father," the pastor earnestly prayed, "watch over those two young men, and see them safely through the ordeal before them."

"Amen," murmured the group of believers.

"What has happened here during the past three days must be kept a secret," the pastor advised. "For their protection as well as ours."

"Only heaven knows what has happened here," spoke up an older man, "and it will remain that way."

On the edge of town, the road sloped gradually downhill making the going easier for Anching who had been struggling with his heavy load.

"Are you all right, Wenpei? I am sorry the road is so bumpy."

From beneath the hay the muffled voice replied, "I'm all right. Don't worry about me. How are you doing? I'm a heavy load to pull."

"You are my brother, and that makes it light," responded Anching as he braced to slow the cart as it picked up speed on the slight downward grade. "We'll make it together with God's help," he said as he struggled to keep control. "Just tell me if you need a rest. When daylight comes, we will not be able to talk to each other because of other people on the road, but just use that rock the pastor gave you to let me know when to stop. Knock three times and I will understand."

"I'm praying that God will strengthen me quickly. You will not be able to pull this load for many days without becoming exhausted."

Conversation lapsed as the sun rose and a steady stream of travelers moved along the dirt road in both directions. Occasionally a truck rumbled by kicking up a cloud of dust that added to Anching's discomfort. For Wenpei under the hay, it became increasingly hot and stifling. Both men longed for a rest and a sip of water.

Speaking only loud enough for Wenpei to hear, he mumbled, "Ah, there's a shady spot ahead. I'm going to stop and rest awhile."

Three knocks came from under the hay as Wenpei signaled his approval.

Responding to the knocks, Anching grunted, "That's what I'll do," as he guided the cart under the tree, and flopped to the ground exhausted.

"Good idea," said a perspiring farmer as he lowered his carrying pole with two large bundles suspended from each end. "It's already getting hot," he said as he sat down next to Anching. "Whew! My load is heavy," he said as he mopped his forehead. "And that load of hay must be heavy also. Where are you going?" he asked.

"Oh, I am delivering this hay to Taiping village up ahead," he replied cautiously. "I slow down when the sun gets high in the sky."

"And so do I," replied the farmer. "You don't talk like one of us," he said as he looked him over. "Where are you from?"

Anching's heart skipped a beat. He didn't expect his speech would give him away as a stranger in the area. He lifted his voice silently in prayer for wisdom. "No," he replied honestly, "I'm not from these parts. A few months ago I had to come this way unexpectedly. I have been living with some friends," he said honestly.

"You must be careful on the road to Taiping," offered the farmer. "The Communist troops swept through this area a few days ago as they routed the government troops. I heard a new battle line has been set up about twenty miles south of here." He paused and looked at Anching with a quizzical look. "What's a young man from a distant province doing in this part of the country?" he asked. Then, without waiting for an answer, he continued, "Don't bother telling me. That's your secret, I think. Better that we don't talk about it," he said with a knowing nod of his head. "Everyone will need to be more careful how they talk from now on," he continued. "I have heard rumors that in areas where the Communists have taken over, they make everyone spy on each other. Have you heard that?"

"I have heard that," Anching replied cautiously, "but I would never spy on my friends or family, no matter what it would cost me."

'Ah, I like you," nodded the farmer. "Your parents must be very proud of you." He paused again, and looked at Anching as he said, "Well, I must be on my way," he said with a friendly wave as he shouldered his heavy load. "Be careful, and stay away from those Communist soldiers, or they might steal your hay." Looking back at Anching as he started back on the road, he gave him a knowing wink.

"That was interesting," Anching said softly as he checked the hay. "Are you okay?" he asked softly. "Maybe the government troops will regroup and fight a rearguard action. That old man said there's fighting two days south of us. At the rate we're going, it will take us another two days at least to reach the front lines. We'll have to be very careful to avoid the area where they're fighting."

"I've been thinking of the Scripture that says 'The steps of a good man are ordered by the Lord.' While you pull, I'm praying for

God's protection and help. You did a good job with that farmer," Wenpei spoke softly. "It won't get easier, but we'll trust in the Lord."

Even though he was rested, Anching moved along the road a bit more slowly than when they started in the morning. His shoulders ached from the strain of the harness, but there was nothing else to do except move forward. The afternoon sun sank lower in the western sky. Every muscle in his body cried out for rest as perspiration flowed freely. *Better look for a good place to spend the night,* he thought as he scanned the landscape ahead. They were the only ones on the road at this point, so he spoke softly to Wenpei. "I see a farm building of some kind ahead. Maybe we can pull in behind it and rest for the night. You must be very weary and stiff."

"I'm doing quite well, but I am concerned for you. You have been pulling this load for almost ten hours already."

"I think I'll feel better after eating some food," he replied. "And that goes for you too, I think."

"That's for sure," he replied. "Those rice balls will taste good."

Anching pulled the cart off to the side of the road. Coming back he spoke to Wenpei. "This looks like a good spot to spend the night. The building is old and dilapidated. We can pull off behind it and not be seen, but you better stay covered until it gets dark. Can't take any chances on being discovered."

The rumble of approaching trucks suddenly awakened both men. In the light of the moon, Anching could make out a convoy of army trucks moving south.

"Reinforcements moving south. That's a bad sign," whispered Anching.

As the sound of the trucks faded in the distance, Wenpei asked, "How do you feel? You must be sore all over," he said sympathetically.

"Well, I must admit I have felt better in my life, but I think I'll survive. It would probably be a good idea to start out and get as far as we can before the sun comes up. It's a lot easier to pull this load when it's cool."

"I'm feeling some better already," Wenpei replied. "How can I ever thank you for what you are doing for me?" he asked.

"You would do the same for me," Anching replied. "I believe we'll make it out safely."

Heading south again, Anching's stiff muscles limbered up and they made good progress along the lonely road. It was still an hour before sunrise as they calculated. Progress was slow indeed, but each mile brought them closer to the railroad where they hoped to find a train going south.

"The pastor said there was a mission hospital in Taiping. Maybe we can reach there by tomorrow at the latest. I would like to have the doctor look at your wounds."

"That may be dangerous. These gunshot wounds will require a lot of explaining, don't you think?"

"You're right," he replied, "but the pastor said we should try and find the missionary first, and see if he can help us. All we can do is trust the Lord and take another step," he replied between breaths as he struggled with a slight incline in the road.

"We'd better stop and have some rice balls," Anching said. "People will be on the road pretty soon, and it will be too dangerous after that."

"The rest and food will do us both good," replied Wenpei. "We won't be able to eat again until dark."

After the brief break they were on the road again, plodding along, step after weary step. By about ten o'clock, the sun was already high in the sky and the temperature was rising, making pulling much more difficult.

"I need to rest," Anching spoke out loud as if to himself. He guided the cart to the side of the road, and slipped out of his harness. He stretched out on the ground and closed his eyes. He was asleep in a few moments. How long he slept he didn't know, but suddenly he was startled by the sound of voices nearby. Sitting up and rubbing his eyes, he saw a young woman seated on the ground nearby nursing a baby. A little child was at her feet crying loudly as if in pain.

"Hello," called Anching as he took in the situation. "Is something wrong with your child?" he asked.

She looked at him with big, tender eyes that reminded him of Meiling. These last few days had been so full of death and fear, he hadn't thought much about her. This young woman brought a flood of memories rushing back. He didn't have long to think of Meiling as he noticed the woman was crying, too.

"You're crying," he said sympathetically. "What's wrong?"

"The fighting," she replied, weeping. "It was awful! My husband was killed in the fighting. He was stationed here with a supply unit. Many wives came and joined their husbands, but we never expected anything like this to happen." She dabbed at her eyes and adjusted the baby. "The post was overrun by Communist troops, and my husband was killed in the battle. I am destitute and alone. My milk has dried up, and my baby and son are hungry. They haven't eaten in two days! I don't know what to do," she said as she broke down into long, heaving sobs.

"I have some rice balls on my cart," Anching said as he got up and walked toward the cart. "Let me get some for you and the children."

Returning with the food, Anching squatted by the little boy who rubbed his eyes in surprise as he watched him open the container.

"Here," he said, "take one."

The little boy grabbed at the food and stuffed his mouth. The sun glistened on the tears still on his cheeks, as his eyes sparkled with renewed hope. The woman chewed up a little food and then pressed it gently into the mouth of her starving baby. It wasn't long before six rice balls had been devoured.

"How can I ever thank you," the young mother said with tears in her eyes. "You are like an angel sent from heaven."

"Not an angel," replied Anching, "but a servant of the Lord Jesus Christ."

"Who is Jesus?" she asked with a big question in her voice.

For the next twenty minutes as the family devoured the rest of the rice balls, Anching told her the story of Jesus.

"I have never heard anything like this before," she admitted as she wiped her little son's face. "But most of all, I don't know how to thank you for what you have done for my children," she said with a relieved smile. "I think now I will be able to make it to my parent's home by tomorrow."

"You can put your children on the cart," replied Anching with a warm smile. "That will make it easier for you to travel."

"Oh, thank you," the woman replied. "And I can help you by pushing," she said gratefully.

This is getting complicated, Anching thought. *I wonder if Wenpei has overheard this conversation? How can I warn him,* he wondered. He lifted the little boy onto the cart as he said, "Sit right here," as he pointed to a spot at the front of the cart. "If you move around, it will make it too hard for me to pull the cart," he explained, "and then you will have to walk with your mother."

"I will sit very still," the little fellow said as he settled in for a comfortable ride.

Anching walked around the cart checking his load as he said to the mother, "Your son can sit up front and the baby can ride here at the back where you can watch him," he said as he tapped the cart. "We should be able to make some good time and help each other."

Wenpei dared not make a sound, but he had heard the whole conversation. *What a man this Anching is,* he thought. *He pulls me through the countryside and now he adds extra weight to the load. And, he does it all because he is a Christian. Lord, help me live in such an unselfish way that I too can help others to know You.*

The afternoon wore on as they made good progress with the mother pushing from behind.

"It is not far until the road divides," she called from the back. "I must bear to the right to reach my parent's home. You will go on to Taiping to the left. This has helped me so much, I will make it to my home early tomorrow," she said with a lilt in her voice. "I don't know how to thank you for your kindness to me."

"I think we must pull over and stop a few minutes," Anching called back. "It looks like there is a road block up ahead and soldiers standing around."

Wenpei heard this news with apprehension. *What can this be all about,* he thought. *Lord,* he prayed, *help us pass through without being discovered.*

As the cart came to a rest, and the mother joined Anching to assess the situation, she commented, "Those are Communist troops at a roadblock. I wonder if they will allow us to pass?" she added anxiously. "You have a foreign accent," she said as she looked at him. "You haven't told me who you are or where you're from. I have been wondering if you are a soldier from the south," she said as she looked Anching directly in the eye. "Could it be that you, too, are a soldier left behind from the battle?" she asked searchingly.

Anching hesitated before answering. She caught the hesitation and nodded, "It's okay. I think I know the answer. I hope you make it through," she said simply, "but this is a dangerous situation up ahead. If you speak, they will recognize your southern accent, and that could spell trouble for both of us. Suppose you let me do the talking. You pretend to be a deaf mute. I will pretend you are my husband and we are taking this hay to my parents. I think I can get us through."

Anching looked at her curiously. "Now, who is the angel?" he asked in amazement. "You are right. My southern accent gives me away, doesn't it? I think you have a good plan."

She smiled. "I will help you escape," she said with a twinkle in her eyes. "After all, we are on the same side. I will walk up front with you from now on," she said, "and when we reach the road block, I will use sign language only. Do not say a word," she ordered. "Let's go. Maybe your God will see us through this difficulty."

"Now it is my turn to be grateful," Anching said. "I do believe God sent you along to help me through this situation."

Anching bent forward and strained against the harness as the cart started moving toward the roadblock.

Turning to her young son, she ordered him not to say a word when they reached the soldiers. "If you do," she said, "they may kill us."

Wenpei realized the seriousness of their situation as he listened to the conversation. *I can't do anything to help them,* he thought *except to pray.* As they approached the roadblock, a soldier ordered them to stop. The mother tapped Anching on the shoulder, and motioned to him to stop. Puffing hard, Anching brought the cart to a stop and stood looking at the soldier.

"Where are you going?" asked the soldier sternly.

The young mother spoke up. "My husband is a deaf mute. He cannot hear your question," she said. "We are going to our home in Shampo Village, about eight miles from here. We bought this hay for our livestock. Please let us pass," she said respectfully.

Several soldiers gathered around the cart, poking at the hay with the butts of their rifles. Wenpei held his breath and prayed.

"This is a very big load of hay," a soldier noticed. "Do you have that many animals to feed?"

Anching prayed for her to give them a good answer. He motioned to her to tell him what was going on. He was a good actor and played his part well.

"Oh, no, this is not only for us," she answered. "We will sell some to our neighbors. It has been difficult to get enough hay for the animals with the war," she said disarmingly.

"Well, you'll have to pay to pass this spot," said the soldier with a wicked grin on his face. "After all, we are fighting to set the country free. We need some payment for our hard work," he laughed.

The others joined in laughing as they held out their hands for money.

Give her wisdom, prayed Anching and Wenpei silently. *You are our refuge and our fortress*, prayed Anching.

"Sirs," replied the woman respectfully, "we paid our last dollars to purchase this hay. We have nothing more to give. Oh, please, let us pass. See, the children are tired and we still have several miles to go."

"You cannot pass without some payment," the soldier replied. "You," he said as he pointed to a young soldier, "take off some of that hay as payment," he ordered.

"Oh, please," cried the woman, "we cannot afford to lose that much."

"Be quiet woman, or we won't let you pass," he said curtly.

She motioned to Anching who looked imploring at the soldier who turned and walked away. Quickly, Anching moved to the side of the cart and began pulling off some of the hay. Just as quickly, he moved to the other side and unloaded more.

"There," said the mother, "you have your hay. Now please let us pass."

"Take some more," a soldier called out. "That's not enough."

"Let them through," ordered the first soldier. "I got what I asked for. That will be enough. Just be careful and stay away from the fighting area."

Anching bent forward into the harness and the cart began to move forward. The mother pushed from behind and they passed through the roadblock safely.

"That was a close one," she said as she pushed hard up the slight grade.

"The Lord was with us and helped us through," Anching replied as he breathed hard. "We'll stop as soon as we reach the top of this grade."

Pulling off to the side, they sat down to rest.

"You came up with a great idea to get us through that barricade, and you did a wonderful job speaking for us," Anching said with a smile of gratitude. "I never played a deaf mute before."

"Well, I was impressed with your acting ability," she answered with a chuckle. "And it was a good thing you acted so quickly to unload those bales from each side of the cart to keep it well balanced," she said with a strange smile on her face. "It would have been a disaster," she continued looking down at the ground, "if those soldiers had taken the hay off and discovered whoever is under the hay," she said as she lifted her eyes to meet his.

"What are you saying?" Anching stammered as shock spread all over his face.

"I know your secret!" she said with a laugh. "When I arranged a place for my baby, and then began to push, I noticed the hay move suspiciously." She paused for effect, enjoying every minute of Anching's surprise and dismay. Before he could recover, she added, "I don't know what this is all about, but I suspected from the beginning that you are a government soldier trying to escape just as we are."

"You're right," Anching slowly confessed. "And, under the hay is my wounded friend, Wenpei. We're trying to reach the hospital in Taiping and then maybe get a train to Shanghai or Hong Kong."

"Well, don't worry about me. I will do everything to help the one who saved my children and me from death."

"As soon as it gets dark, we'll pull over for the night, and get some food, and then I'll introduce you to my friend. But for now, we'd better keep moving and find a good place to camp."

"I know just the place," she responded happily. "A short distance ahead, right on this road, I have a very trustworthy uncle. We'll be able to stay with them tonight. They'll also make us a good meal. You men deserve one after your long trip. Tomorrow I will easily make it home, thanks to you. I will be so glad to be back with my family at last after all these horrible experiences."

"I am just glad that the Lord caused our paths to cross, and we were able to help each other. And, I hope you will some day know the peace of God in your heart as we do. That would make these experiences worthwhile," he replied.

As they pulled over for a rest, Anching said, "Come and meet Wenpei. He was wounded in the shoulder at that last battle," he said as he pulled some hay aside and introduced the two.

"I heard your whole conversation," Wenpei said as soon as introductions were over. "You two did a superb job back at the roadblock. I was really scared for a few moments when it looked like our secret would be discovered."

"That was a close one," agreed Anching, "but thank God He has been watching over us and delivering us from the enemy."

"We will get your wounds dressed this evening," the mother said as she tucked her baby in the hay. "Now we'd better get moving, or we won't make it by dark."

Anching smiled as he laid into the harness again and began to move forward.

Three hours later, they reached the top of the grade and looked down the road to an isolated farmhouse surrounded by wheat fields.

"That's my uncle's home," the mother said as they rested a few moments at the top of the grade. "We'll be safe there tonight. Don't worry about my family. They despise the Communists and all they stand for."

A few minutes later, they pulled up in front of the house. The mother and her children rushed in and told the story of the battle and her husband's death. "It is a miracle that I am here safe and sound," she said as her auntie bounced the baby with great delight. "What are we waiting for?" her husband said. "Where is the man who saved you?"

"Welcome, young man," he said joyfully. "I understand you saved my niece and her children. You are welcome to stay here and rest a while. Mother," he said, "prepare a meal. They must all be famished."

When the meal was over and Wenpei's wound was washed and dressed, Anching spoke from his heart. "Your kindness has overwhelmed us," he began. "We must leave before dawn in the morning. No one must know that we stayed here tonight, or your lives will be in danger."

"Wenpei is not ready to leave so quickly," the auntie replied. "Just remain here for one or two days so I can feed you and help you both get strong again."

"Anching is right," spoke up Wenpei. "We would only cause you future trouble if anyone discovered you helped us. You have already done us a great service and we thank you, but we will leave while it is still dark."

"What a crime," exclaimed the uncle. "Those Communists will ruin our country," he said vehemently, "but I believe you are right. Go to sleep now and rest as much as you can. It will soon be time to leave."

The young mother looked tearful as she thanked Anching for his kindness. "I will never forget you," she said, "and I will seek the God you have spoken of. I want the same peace in my heart that you have."

"Here is my New Testament," Anching said as he held out the book to her. "Read it and ask the living God to open your understanding. If you seek Jesus, you will find Him just as we did. And we will pray for you and your family. Maybe someday we will meet again when China's night is past, but if not, we will look for you in heaven." "I will be there," she answered simply. "I know you have spoken

God's truth to me, and I will follow Him," she said with confidence. "Are there any Christians in your village?" Anching asked. "No, there are none, but I have heard there are some in the next village. I will seek them out and learn more about Jesus," she promised.

Long before daybreak, Anching and Wenpei started down the road toward Taiping with enough food to last them for the journey.

"The Lord led us," said Anching as he pulled the cart. "And He led us to that young mother. I expect to meet her in heaven some day."

"That's for sure," Wenpei replied. "And I'm feeling stronger after the good food and rest we had. This will be my last day in the cart. The pain has ceased unless I bump my shoulder."

As dusk began to gather, Anching looked ahead to the outskirts of Taiping.

"Ah, at last I see the town," he said. "I will ask directions to the hospital as soon as I meet someone," he said. "Thank God, we have arrived here safely. But don't stop praying, Wenpei. We still have some problems to overcome. The first is, we must find the missionary."

As they reached the edge of town, Anching saw a small wayside eating place—nothing more than a table and a bench at the front of a rundown looking building. An old man was sitting at the table drinking tea with a friend. Anching pulled the cart to the side of the road, walked over, and sat down.

"Here, have some tea," the old man said with a friendly gesture. "Where are you going with that load of hay?"

"I am headed to the Christian hospital," he began. "I need to speak with the foreign doctor and deliver this load of hay," he replied. "Can you tell me where it is located?"

"Why, of course," he replied. "Follow me. I work for the doctor as his gatekeeper."

"Oh, praise the Lord," Anching exclaimed happily.

"Oh, you must be a believer!" responded the old man with a toothless grin.

"Yes, indeed I am," he replied.

"And are you taking this hay to the doctor?" the old man asked in surprise.

"That is what I was told to do," Anching replied, hoping to avoid more questions.

A half-hour later, as they approached the doctor's home, the old gatekeeper said, "I will inform the doctor that you are here. Is he expecting you? Who shall I say wants to see him? he asked.

"Just tell him that the pastor from Panfu sent me to him on an urgent mission."

"Just as you say," said the old man as he entered the courtyard of the doctor's home.

A few minutes later, a tall, handsome man in his forties appeared, followed by the gatekeeper. Speaking in very good Mandarin he asked, "I am Dr. Hanson. Do you have an urgent message for me from the pastor in Panfu?"

"Yes, I do," replied Anching, "but I must speak with you privately."

"Come in, come in," he replied. "Han," he said to the old man, "watch our friend's load of hay for a few minutes while I talk with him inside."

"Don't worry, young man," the gatekeeper said. "I am the best watchman in this city," he said as he smiled his toothless smile again.

"And that you are, Han," replied the doctor. "Now young man, come on inside and tell me what this is all about."

"Doctor," began Anching carefully, "the pastor in Panfu told me to find you and see if you could help me."

"Please, do not be agitated or afraid," the doctor replied. "Han tells me you are a believer. That is good. Our Lord has placed me here to help those in need. Tell me, what is troubling you?"

Anching spent the next ten minutes telling his story and why he was at the hospital.

"You have a serious problem," the doctor responded as Anching finished. "But you've come to the right place. First, I must get your friend inside and look at his wound. Then, we will decide what to do next."

Leading the way out to the cart, he said to Anching, "Han is one of the most trusted men I have ever met. He will help us get your friend inside and take care of the load of hay."

"Oh, thank you doctor," Anching replied with much relief. "It has been a long, hard journey, but God has led me all the way."

"And He will lead you on, never fear. He specializes in doing impossible things," replied Dr. Hanson.

After conferring with Han for a few minutes, the doctor returned. "Pull the cart around to the back of the property. It is secluded back there. Your friend can get out and come in the back gate. Han will take care of the hay."

A few minutes later, Anching and Wenpei were ushered into the doctor's home.

"My wife will prepare some food for you," he said with a smile. "I don't suppose you have eaten all day."

"That's true," replied Anching, "but we did have a very good meal with the farmer where we stayed last night."

"Well, my wife is a good cook, too as you'll see in just a little while. Now, let me look at this wound."

"Those bullets came close to your heart, young man," he said as he examined Wenpei's shoulder. "It was the mercy of God that you are alive. I must say that whoever cared for you did a fine job. I believe you will make a full recovery."

With the wounded shoulder cleaned and dressed, he said, "And now it is time to eat."

"Thank you, doctor," Anching replied, "but before we eat, we want to thank you for your kindness to us. You have placed yourself in jeopardy by taking us in. I am afraid that the Communist troops will soon overrun this town, too, and that could make it dangerous for you."

"I know," replied the doctor, "but if we avoid doing what is right and helping people, especially those of God's family, we would be dishonoring our God. My wife and I are prepared for whatever happens; even death for Jesus' sake. Now, let's see. There is a train leaving for Canton in the morning. We will try and get you on board without anyone knowing you were here tonight. Now come, have some good food and get some rest. It is the Lord who watches over all of us and uses us to help others find their way to Him."

Chapter 8

NIGHT FALLS

A s 1950 dawned over the troubled land of China, the sinister clouds hanging low on the horizon broke loose in a down pour of sorrow and death. The dark shadows crept over the land, and a night of death and oppression descended everywhere. A way of life, long cherished by the Chinese, began to disappear as the grip of terror settled on every community. Wherever the Communists gained control they instituted new and frightening regulations designed to cause everyone to become a spy for the government. No one was exempt and no subject was off limits. Children were taught to report on their parents, and parents on neighbors and even friends.

With the defeat of government forces in the decisive battle that turned the tide of the war, Mao Zedong tightened his grip on every city, town, and hamlet. Anching and Wenpei finally made their way to crowded Hong Kong. Along with thousands of former soldiers and other refugees, they swarmed into the refuge of the British colony. Breathing with relief that they had made it safely, they little realized how cruel and hard life would be for them as refugees.

Back in Puyang, the noose was tightening on those considered capitalists, the educated, and anyone who opposed the harsh decrees the government laid down. Mr. Pang's plastics factory slowed down only because there were constant shortages of supplies due to disrupted transportation and the chaos of war. And then, there was the new presence of the political advisor appointed to oversee the workers. He had not been chosen because of his superior knowledge of manufacturing, but because he was a fanatically faithful Communist party member. He had the power to overrule everyone in charge at the factory, including Pang, the owner.

Comrade Sung exercised his newly gained authority especially over Pang. He had a sadistic streak in him that thoroughly enjoyed making the older man twist and squirm in humiliation. Every evening after the long workday, all the workers were ordered to attend political indoctrination classes for two interminable hours. No one was excused, and no one dared to fall asleep or miss a meeting.

At one such meeting, Comrade Sung began his familiar tirade.

"Tonight, we will examine the policies that have governed this factory under the old feudal system," stated Sung as he looked over at Pang seated in the front row. "Everyone knows that the workers have been mistreated by these imperialistic capitalists who have stuffed their pockets at our expense," he continued, glaring at Pang. "Take, for example, the way Pang has become rich while paying you such a miserably small salary. How many of you have a limousine at your disposal, or a large home with servants?"

He looked around for effect as Pang squirmed uncomfortably. The workers nodded their heads in agreement, and that encouraged Sung to move on to his next point.

"Don't you all agree that Pang, who has gotten his riches illegally from the workers, should be punished for his crimes?"

The sleepy people sat up at attention at this unexpected turn of events. They listened intently as Sung droned on about the excesses of evil perpetrated by Pang. Pointing to a foreman on the front row, he asked in a commanding tone of voice, "Don't you agree that he should be fined $500,000 yuan [Chinese money] for his crimes?"

The surprised man shot fearful glances at the other foremen. What should he say? There was no help from the others. They just sat there stunned by the judgment falling on poor Pang.

"Answer me," shouted Sung angrily. "You have been abused by this man, have you not? You have been cheated out of fair wages, have you not?" he bellowed. The frightened man gave a slight nod of his head, not knowing what else to do.

"Yes, he says," announced Sung triumphantly. "Pang, stand to your feet and face the people's workers."

Trembling from head to foot, Pang stood and with bowed head stood before the workers and listened to Sung rant about the supposed abuses.

"For these abuses that have deprived the workers of just wages, you are fined 500,000 yuan to be paid by noon tomorrow in my office," he pronounced with evident satisfaction. "You are all dismissed.

The workers filed out silently; stunned. Only in the privacy of their homes did they dare to talk quietly behind closed doors. Though they had no great affection for Pang, they all felt the sting of this unjust treatment, and they trembled. They suddenly realized they could be next in line.

Pang returned to his home in a state of shock and agitation. There was no justice in what was happening. He had not been given any opportunity to defend himself, and the fine was imposed by Sung alone. "Where will this end?" he asked his frightened wife. "The way things are going, Sung will not rest until I have been stripped from all authority in my own factory. I am afraid of what the future holds for us," he admitted fearfully.

The report of the factory meeting and the humiliation of Mr. Pang soon reached the ears of everyone in Puyang. Each night, at the indoctrination classes required of everyone in the factory, workers from the lowest ranks spouted off about the supposed abuses of the former government and how the Communist regime would restore the workers to their rightful place of control. In spite of the rhetoric, none of the workers saw any changes in their wages or living conditions. What they did experience was a tightening of control on every thought they had, and the need to report on family and neighbors in order to gain a little extra ration of food.

Mr. Woo spoke guardedly to his wife in the secrecy of their inner room.

"We are witnessing the end of our liberties," he said quietly to his wife. "Before long they will come after me, and our family will suffer just like Pang is suffering. We will need to be careful what we say even around our home because our children will be grilled before long and forced to make statements they do not believe."

"Do you really think it will come to that?" asked his wife with quivering voice. "What have you done to deserve such humiliation and punishment?"

"We belong to the educated class," he replied. "The Communists are determined to destroy us and create a new society."

"Do you think it will affect the church and Pastor Yang and the believers?" she asked.

"Without a doubt, they will be included. Communists are atheists. They say that religion is the opiate of the people. They boldly declare there is no God and I suspect they will use every imaginable method to enforce their views."

"My poor children," cried Mrs. Woo softly. "What have they done to deserve this?"

The next evening, as the family finished their evening meal, Mr. Woo spoke softly to his children.

"My dear family," he began, "I must share some thoughts with you tonight about the events that are happening in our city and country." Everyone gave special attention to him as he spoke. "The events that have happened to Mr. Pang may soon affect us as a family, also."

"What do you mean, Father?" asked Meiling anxiously. "Do you think you will be placed on trial and humiliated as Mr. Pang was?"

He paused in deep thought before replying. "I believe I will be," he said sadly. "And it will affect us all," he said as he looked at each one in the circle. "But we must be strong and honorable in the face of the difficulties ahead of us."

Meiling interrupted her father, and said, "Father, we are family. We will stand together no matter what happens. With God's help, I will never bring disgrace on you or our family, and I am sure I speak for our entire family." She glanced around the table at her brothers and sisters who nodded silently. "I know also that we are going to face the wrath of the Communists because we are considered intellectuals, and furthermore, we are Christians." She paused a moment and gave her father an opportunity to object, but after waiting a moment without any protest, she continued, "Because we are Christians, we can expect to suffer persecution, and maybe even death." She paused, expecting to hear the familiar protest from her father. Hearing none, she concluded with conviction, "And I for one am ready to lay down my life for Jesus."

Tears flooded Mr. Woo's eyes as each of his children reiterated the same sentiment.

"My dear children," he stammered, "you are a great joy to your mother and me. The days ahead will be very difficult and we will be pressed to the point of despair. We may be called upon to testify against each other in a struggle meeting, but I am encouraged that we will be strong and the Lord will help us. I have not said this before, but as you know, I have been reading the Bible and I am finding much help in the words of Jesus. I can't say that I am a believer yet, but I am praying to find my way to God."

This statement was greeted with joyous laughter and clapping of hands.

"Oh, Father, that's wonderful news," Meiling said with a delighted smile. "We will stand on the promises of God and draw our help and our strength from Him. He will be there when we need Him most, and Satan will not be able to overcome us."

"I believe that," Mr. Woo said simply as tears filled everyone's eyes.

Several weeks passed without further incident at the factory, although Pang felt the intense pressure creeping up on him. It was a Tuesday morning when he arrived at the factory and observed workers gathered around the new bulletin board that had been erected. They moved away silently as Pang arrived. Walking over to see what had attracted the workers, he was filled with consternation as he read that tomorrow night all workers would be required to appear at a meeting to determine whether he should relinquish control of the factory.

Sung was standing nearby observing his reaction. A sadistic smirk spread across his pudgy face as Pang glanced in his direction. Sung waved his hand in greeting and called over authoritatively, "Be there. It is important." Pang walked quickly to his office, closed the door, and locked it. A strange feeling swept over him that this was his last day in his factory! He buried his face in his hands and sobbed at the prospects of the uncertain future.

The workers gathered in silence in the cafeteria that had been rearranged for the evening's meeting. An improvised platform had been erected at one end of the room with just a small table placed in the center and a longer one off to the side facing the audience. The starkness of the room made it seem more ominous as the workers sat silently, wondering what was about to take place. Pang entered the room and walked to the front, taking a seat a low-level worker indicated was reserved for him. A quiet murmur passed through the audience as he took his seat. Soon three men in Mao jackets solemnly entered the room and took their places at the long table. A deathly silence settled on the crowd as they anticipated the entrance of Comrade Sung. After allowing the suspense to build for a few minutes, he appeared from a side door with gavel in hand and took his place at the table in the center of the platform. Lifting the gavel, he pounded the table vigorously. It was unnecessary, since silence already reigned, but he did so deliberately to let it be known that he was in charge.

Opening the folder he brought with him, he announced pompously, "Workers of the Peaceful Heaven Plastics Factory [the new name he had given the factory], we have gathered here this evening to determine who is best qualified to lead this factory—Pang Maching or you, the workers." He paused for effect before continuing in a harsh voice, "The defendant will rise and come to the platform. He will kneel before the workers and only answer the questions he is asked."

Pang got to his feet unsteadily and slowly approached the platform. Turning to face the workers with downcast eyes, he hesitated a moment. A Communist worker standing nearby pushed him roughly to his knees. Pain shot through his legs as he fell to his knees, causing him to gasp audibly, much to the delight of Sung. Pang moved from knee to knee as he fought back the pain.

Sung stood, and turning to the three judges seated on the platform, he began to read the charges. Speaking in a clear, unwavering voice he announced, "Pang Maching, the capitalist who owns Peaceful Heaven Plastics Factory, is charged with three serious charges against the workers of this factory." He paused and looked at Pang who was painfully shifting from knee to knee, and then he continued. "Charge number one. The output of the factory is down thirty percent from one year ago," he intoned. "Charge number two," he continued. "Pang has neglected to make the factory safe for his workers and some have suffered serious injury. Charge number three," he said, "is the most serious. He has given comfort and aid to the enemy, the Nationalist army, by bribing them with a large gift of 7,000 yuan.

"This," intoned Sung, "is considered treason, and worthy of the severest punishment."

Hearing the last charge, Pang wobbled on his knees and pain seared through his body like bolts of lightning. Unable to stand the pain any longer, he collapsed and rolled to the floor with his back toward Sung. Enraged, Sung jumped to his feet, screaming at Pang for his disrespect at turning his back to him. He viciously kicked him, again and again. With each kick, Pang cried out in pain, as everyone in the room stiffened in shock.

"How dare you turn your back to me," Sung shouted in anger. "Get to your knees," he screamed as he gave him another vicious kick. He ordered the cadres to get him to his knees. They struggled with his excessive weight, but managed to drag him to a kneeling position again.

"We will call for witnesses on each of the charges," announced Sung, puffing from his anger and exertion. "The first witness is Wen Puwah, day foreman, and trusted employee of Peaceful Heaven Plastics Factory."

Wen stood to his feet and faced Sung and the judges. His heart pounded madly as he tried to clear his mind. Not since Anching was forced to leave home had he been faced with such a situation. He sensed danger lurking everywhere as if ready to pounce on him and devour him. He licked his lips nervously as every eye focused on him. In the few suspenseful moments afforded him as he stood to his feet, he pondered his situation. *How to be loyal to Mr. Pang while at the same time not saying things that would incriminate him.*

He didn't have long to wait.

"Wen Puwah," Sung announced in a pompous voice, "tell the court that the production is down thirty percent from last year."

Wen's tongue seemed stuck to the roof of his mouth as he tried to answer. Nervously rubbing his hands together, he gathered courage and strength to reply. "Comrade Sung, our supply of raw materials was down considerably because of the disruption of . . ."

"Answer the question, Wen," shouted an angry Sung, "without excuses. Is production down by thirty percent this year or not?"

"Yes, it is," stammered Wen, "but . . ."

"No buts," shouted Sung. "Was there a thirty percent reduction in productivity? Answer me and tell the court," he said as he gritted his teeth and glared at Wen.

"Production is down thirty percent," he replied in a whisper as he hung his head in shame.

"Thank you. You may be seated," said Sung. "On charge number two concerning safety in the plant, I call the factory gatekeeper to the stand."

An old man whose job it was to open and close the gates as vehicles came and went stood shakily to his feet.

"Tell the court how you were injured at the front gate," ordered Sung.

The old man looked at Pang who was suffering intense pain on his knees.

He remembered the many kind things Pang had done for him and the extra tip he received last New Year's.

Trembling, the old man began, "I have worked for Mr. Pang for more than thirty years," he started. "Last year he gave me a generous tip at New Year's and helped me when my hand was injured when a truck hit the gate."

Sung jumped to his feet and pounded the table with his gavel. "You will answer the question, do you understand?" he bellowed. "Did Pang replace the gate after the accident?"

"It was not necessary to do so," replied the old man defiantly. "It was repaired promptly. The problem was not a poor gate, but a poor driver who caused the accident."

A young female cadre standing nearby walked up to the old man and slapped him in the face as she ordered him only to answer Comrade Sung's question.

Sung remained standing as he waited for the answer he wanted. As the old gatekeeper was slow in responding, Sung announced, "The witness suffered a serious accident and the gate was not replaced, thus making it a serious crime that imperiled the safety of the workers of this factory. You may take your seat. We will now consider the most serious of the crimes, the one of treason—giving money to the enemy."

Pang's whole body was trembling with fear and pain as he realized what was happening to him. He gathered his last ounce of strength and courage, and raising his head, he looked directly at Sung. "I have never committed treason of any kind nor have I helped the enemy. I did not give comfort money to any government troops. I simply paid for the release of my son from the army as so many others have done." Having said that, he swayed uncertainly on his aching knees, and then slumped to the floor as severe cramps crippled him with agonizing pain.

A young cadre picked up a whip and struck Pang across the back, again and again. The crowd shuddered as they watched in horrified silence. The old gatekeeper rose in an attempt to prevent the beating, but another cadre roughly pushed him back into his seat.

"Give him thirty lashes for his insolence to the court," ordered Sung as blow after blow landed on Pang's crumpled body.

Heartlessly watching the beating of the helpless man, Sung waited until all thirty strokes had been administered. Turning to the judges he announced that all the witnesses had spoken and he would rest the case. The three judges immediately went into a huddle on the platform and in three minutes stood to announce they had reached a unanimous verdict. "Guilty beyond a shadow of a doubt," one announced. "The penalty for these crimes against the People's Republic of China and the workers of Peaceful Heaven Plastics Factory is death."

The crowd gasped. Mrs. Pang who had entered quietly with her son, Luping, just before the proceedings had begun, slumped to the floor in a faint. No one dared to help her, not even Luping. He sat motionless as he stared at his father's broken body lying in a heap. This was not the new China he had anticipated. He wished he had the courage to stand and defend his father. Instead he sat motionless, lest he too be beaten and killed. Mrs. Pang stirred on the floor, but he did nothing to help her. Like everyone else in the room, he was learning fast that to survive, one surrendered all loyalty to family and friends.

Sung stood and smiled triumphantly as he said to the workers, "Let this be an example to everyone here tonight. Those who insist on fighting against the People's Republic will suffer the consequences. The sentence of the court will be carried out immediately. Everyone, remain in your seats and under no circumstance cause any disturbance," he announced gruffly.

A cadre produced a rope and strung it through the hook already prepared in the ceiling. This kangaroo court had no intention of seeking justice for Pang. The intention was pre-determined: remove him from ownership of his factory and make him a frightening example of what happens to those who oppose the new regime. Wire was produced and twisted around each of Pang's thumbs, and then tied to the rope. Two strong cadres yanked on the rope, pulling Pang's heavy body into the air by his thumbs. The onlookers gasped at this barbaric torture. Stunned, the crowd sat motionless as if glued to their seats as Pang's body swayed from his thumbs. At the first jerk, what little life was left in Pang after the kicking and beating brought forth only a weak scream as pain shot through every part of his body.

Comrade Sung, enjoying his triumph, continued to harangue the crowd as they stared at the swaying body writhing in agony. A half-hour later, they were excused with the admonition that in the New China, the state would eliminate all capitalists and those who dared oppose the state and the workers' paradise.

Long after the building emptied of shocked and frightened workers, Wen and the old gatekeeper, stood silently outside the door in the shadows wondering what they could do for Mr. Pang. Seeing no one around, they finally entered the building and carefully lowered his lifeless body to the floor.

"He's dead," confirmed Wen as he tried to find a pulse. "This is murder, clear and simple, performed right before the eyes of hundreds of workers," he said as he broke down and wept openly. "What has happened to our country and our people?" he asked between sobs.

"I have a cart nearby." With much grunting and effort, they finally succeeded in getting the lifeless body on the cart.

"Now go," commanded the gatekeeper in a strong voice. "I will take his body to his home. I am an old man, and I have lived many years, but you are still young. China will need strong men to fight this evil that has come to our land. You go home. I will do the rest."

Wen protested, but the old man stopped his ears. "Do as I say. You are a good man, and your family will need you. You helped take the body down. Now I will do the rest."

Wen realized the wisdom in the old man's advice. Sadly waving good-bye to his friend, he slipped away in the darkness. Quickly he moved along the deserted streets to his home. It was as if everyone knew what had happened at the factory and all were securely behind locked doors. Reaching his home, his wife looked at him and cried out in fright, "What's the matter? What happened at the factory tonight?"

Wen sat down and buried his face in his hands as his shoulders shook with sobs.

His wife had never seen him act this way before, not even when Anching had been taken. She placed her hand on his shoulder and waited.

Finally, after many minutes of sobbing, he lifted his head and said, "That man Sung, the political boss of the factory, conducted a mock court tonight and condemned Pang to death. They hung him by his thumbs and we were all forced to watch."

Mrs. Wen dropped to her knees at his side, and though they seldom showed any signs of emotion in their relationship as husband and wife, she stroked his shoulder and began to weep as she said softly, "Oh, my God, help us."

Gradually, Wen told her the whole gruesome story of the hanging and what he and the gatekeeper had done.

"I am proud of you," she said with a nod of approval. "You are an honorable man. That was very dangerous to do, but our God will help us and protect us."

"Do not tell the children," he said. "It might put them in a difficult situation if they are questioned. If they are questioned in school about Mr. Pang's body, they will not have to make any excuses. I think that will be best."

"I agree," she said simply as she wiped her eyes. In her heart though she wondered where all of this would lead them, and what price they would have to pay.

Chapter 9

....

A TIME OF TESTING

With the occupation of the major industrial region of Wuhan in Central China completed, including the cities of Hankou, Hanyang, and Wuchang, the army was free to move southward. Gloom settled over the cities as one new restriction after another was enacted with a harshness never experienced under the Nationalist government. Factories, schools, and the churches began to feel the tightening of the noose as liberties once enjoyed were taken away.

When Pastor Yang received the notice that he, his wife, and staff members of the church were to meet at a large church in Hankou for a meeting of all church staff, he looked at his wife with furrowed brow and said to her, "Now we will begin to feel the sting of the dragon. This meeting will not be good for us or the church."

"I believe you are right," replied Mrs. Yang. "We will feel the sting of that old dragon, Satan, but we must always remember that he is a defeated foe. He may rant and terrify the church, but he will never be able to overcome it."

Pastor Yang looked at his wife with admiration. "You are so right, my dear wife, but we must be prepared for a time of testing such as we have never experienced before. The promises of God have never failed. From now on, we will be sustained by those promises when there is nothing left to lean on."

On the day of the meeting, pastors and staff people assembled in the large auditorium in Hankou, just across the river from Puyang, the suburb of Wuchang. There was a sense of apprehension in the air for everyone sensed that the ax was about to fall. Each struggled with his or her thoughts on how to react.

A hush fell over the audience as the commanding office of the region walked on to the platform flanked by the political director and other Communist dignitaries. The number of high ranking officials and the pomp of the occasion was not lost on the pastors. They waited expectantly as the new national anthem was played and the Communist flag unfurled. The commanding officer stepped to the podium and gave a rousing speech. He praised his army for the great achievement of liberating the country from the corruption of the Nationalist thugs who had fled to Taiwan.

Everyone waited with bated breath for the speech of the political czar of the area, to learn the fate of the church under the Communists. He stepped to the podium amid polite applause and began the speech that would change the way the church operated for many years to come.

"Pastors and staff workers of the churches of the Wuhan area, I come before you today to inform you of new policies of the People's Republic of China that have been designed for the good of all the people. We will soon be appointing a regional Religious Affairs Bureau that will give guidance to all religious affairs in the province and carry out the directives of the Communist Party on behalf of all the newly liberated workers of this province."

Tension started building as the man continued to outline some of the duties of the Religious Affairs Bureau and how they would affect the church. Most of the people gathered sat silently as they anticipated the penalty for refusing to bring the church under the state. There was no doubt that the next months would become increasingly difficult to carry on church activities as before. Consternation filled them as the political leader warmed to the heart of his speech.

"Now that the People's Republic of China has ousted the Nationalist thugs and the missionaries of those foreign imperialist nations who have enslaved the Chinese people for decades, we will assume the training of all children through age eighteen in the teachings of our revered Chairman Mao. In order to do that, all churches will immediately cease instruction of children in schools and churches. Those who cooperate will be able to continue with other meetings, but it should be noted that the People's Republic will not tolerate any opposition to this policy."

He paused for effect as the implications of this new edict registered on all present. Furtive glances were cast at one another, but no sound came from the people. They waited anxiously for what was yet to come.

"Concerning the content of your sermons," he intoned with a sinister air, "please take careful note. The content will be subject to the approval of the Religious Affairs Bureau without exception. You will uphold all the principles of the Communist Party that will be circulated to you soon, and you will use your position as pastor and staff to propagate these policies that have been designed for the good of the people. Again, those who cooperate with the Religious Affairs Bureau will be able to continue their activities." He paused again for effect before continuing. "Those who are stubborn and unwilling to learn and support these policies will be required to attend re-education classes. My advice to each one is to carefully seek to understand the policies that will be circulated to you and conform to them."

The pastors stirred restlessly as the man ended his speech with this sinister threat. Silence reigned for a few uncertain seconds as the audience calculated the risks involved. A sympathetic supporter broke the silence as he stood to his feet and began clapping. One after another, a few people stood slowly and uncertainly, but most just clapped politely and remained seated.

In a pre-arranged scenario, the pastor of a large and influential church rose and walked to the platform where he praised the speeches of these leaders as well as the far-sighted plans and policies of the Party to bring China out of the darkness of feudalism. Different pastors took the cue and rose to praise the party, and save their necks.

Mrs. Yang leaned closer to her husband and whispered, "You must speak up for Jesus," she said emphatically. "He is being denied by these men who are simply seeking to save themselves. It is a disgrace to the cause of Jesus Christ," she added vehemently.

"If I speak," he whispered back, "you will be a widow."

Looking at her husband, she responded, "I would rather be a widow than the wife of a man who denied his Lord."

Strengthened by these words, he rose confidently to his feet and walked with head erect to the podium. Most people in the audience knew him as a godly man who upheld the Bible as the authoritative Word of God. They waited anxiously to hear what he would say.

"Brethren," he began slowly, "we have listened to the speeches of our new leaders who have outlined the new policies that will affect our work in the church. We are instructed in the Bible to respect the authorities God has placed over us, and I will."

The political czar smiled broadly and nodded his head in approval. The audience of pastors, however, listened attentively, and with some trepidation as they sensed that Pastor Yang was about to make a statement that would draw the line. The Communist leaders waited uneasily, although the beginning statement pleased them. They leaned forward slightly to catch every nuance of his words. They had been forewarned that this man was a popular leader who would bring the first challenge to the new regime.

Bracing himself for his next statement, and breathing a prayer for wisdom, he continued, "The Bible also says that we must obey God rather than man in matters of conscience and our allegiance to Jesus Christ. In the church I serve, we will obey the commands of government that are not in conflict with the Bible, but I must take my stand here before you all today, and inform you that I will never deny my Lord. No matter what the consequences may be, I will faithfully follow Jesus and serve Him with my whole heart."

He turned and walked off the platform amid deafening silence as each pastor contemplated the effect of those words. Suddenly, the whole auditorium burst into enthusiastic applause as the political leader rushed to the podium and with raised hands, attempted to silence the crowd. With anger flushing his face, he stormed and ranted as the audience quieted as quickly as it had erupted in applause.

"You will do well to follow the advice of the first speakers," he warned ominously. "The state will help you understand the policies, if necessary, through re-education," he concluded as he brought the meeting to an end.

Mrs. Yang looked at her husband and with quivering voice she whispered, "Both Jesus and I are happy with your stand. It will be very difficult for us, but we will never deny our Lord, and in the end, He will vindicate us and bless our testimony."

As the Yangs moved out of the auditorium, several other pastors came by and whispered, "Amen, brother, we will do the same."

The pastor from the large church was waiting at the door as Pastor Yang approached. With a smirk on his face, he said, "Yang, that was very unwise. Reconsider your position or you will surely feel the sting of re-education. Think of your family and your flock. Do not desert them at this time."

Pastor Yang replied with a wistful sound to his voice, "My friend, I pity you. You may have saved your neck for a while, but you will lose your soul in the end." He continued on out the door knowing full well, that sooner or later, he would be called in for questioning.

Several weeks passed with no apparent changes being enforced. At Pastor Yang's church, they discontinued Sunday school and all instruction to children in compliance with the new rules, but he carefully explained to parents what their responsibilities were before God.

"Now is the time to live your lives in such a way that your children will never misunderstand your love for Jesus. Pray with them and for them, so that when persecution arises, you all will be able to stand the test. For those who do, God has great rewards that no government can prevent from being poured out on you and your family."

He spent much time in prayer for wisdom and courage to be given to him and his wife. He packed a small bag with essentials and prepared for the inevitable visit from the police. One October Sunday morning dawned clear and bright as he prepared for the service. The believers were faithfully gathering week by week for worship and prayer meetings, and today was no exception. They greeted him warmly as they entered the building in expectation of a heart-warming message of comfort and hope.

The singing of Martin Luther's great hymn, *A Mighty Fortress* ended on a triumphant note as the congregation settled down to the preaching of the Word. He opened his Bible to Matthew 16 and read the story of Peter's confession of Jesus. With joy he read,

"Simon Peter answered, 'You are the Christ, the Son of the living God.' Jesus replied, 'Blessed are you, Simon son of Jonah, for this was not revealed to you by man, but by my Father in heaven. And I tell you that you are Peter, and on this rock I will build my church, and the gates of hell will not overcome it.'"

He was well into his message, giving a ringing testimony of his faith in Jesus and the ultimate victory of His kingdom, when a loud commotion erupted at the entrance to the sanctuary crowded with people. Police officers with batons raised rushed up to the platform and roughly grabbed Pastor Yang. The congregation gasped in utter shock.

"You are breaking the law by speaking as you are today," shouted the captain as his men twisted Yang's arms behind him and clamped on handcuffs. With a vicious swing, the captain struck Yang on the side of his head with his baton, causing him to reel and almost lose his balance. "You are under arrest," he continued, "for breaking the law. This sermon has not been submitted to the Religious Affairs Bureau for approval." As he shoved him off the platform he said, "You are all dismissed, and be warned that those who break the law will be punished."

"Where are you taking our pastor," spoke up a courageous elder as he blocked the aisle. "He has done nothing but read the Holy Bible to us."

The policeman nearest him struck a blow to his face and shoved him violently back into his seat. No one ever remembered when they had ever seen a young policeman strike an elder like this before. A wave of protest started as a murmur at first, but it grew louder by the minute, until the captain pulled out his pistol and shot into the air three or four times. Silence fell on the people.

"You will not challenge the authority of the People's Republic of China," he shouted. "Those who do will suffer the consequences."

Pushing and pulling Pastor Yang, they headed out of the church.

"You have five minutes to prepare some things you want to take with you," one of the officers said curtly.

"I have been expecting you," replied Pastor Yang quietly. "My bag is all packed."

As Mrs. Yang hastily brought his little bag, she whispered to him, "The Lord is our strength and refuge in times of trouble. Be strong and courageous in the Lord and honor Him."

"By God's grace, I will," he said simply as he walked away with the police.

As he was entering the police van waiting for him, his heart was warmed as the congregation burst into singing, *How Firm A Foundation*. Pastor Yang heard the words distinctly as they sang.

How firm a foundation, ye saints of the Lord,
Is laid for your faith in His excellent word.
What more can He say, than to you He hath said,
To you who for refuge to Jesus have fled?

Fear not, I am with thee, O be not dismayed,
For I am thy God and will still give thee aid.
I'll strengthen thee, help thee, and cause thee to stand
Upheld by My righteous, omnipotent hand.

The door of the van slammed shut, but Pastor Yang had gotten the message from his courageous congregation. He sang along with them, and suffered another blow to his face that cut his lips, but his heart overflowed with joy.

Mrs. Yang sadly watched the van pull away with her husband. *O Lord, protect Your servant and give him courage to endure what-*

ever they do to him, and bring him back soon, she prayed. Going back into the church as the singing of the great hymn ended, she walked quietly to the platform and reported what had happened to her husband.

"He has been called upon to be a witness for Jesus," she began with quivering voice. "This will not be an easy time for my husband, but with your prayers supporting him, he will be able to endure with the help of the Lord. Now, we must all be faithful to the Lord, and ask God to cause His Word to flourish in spite of this persecution."

"Amen," said the elder who had been struck by the police officer. "Now brothers and sisters," he continued, "let us pray for our pastor that God will sustain him, and for ourselves that we will be faithful." He then led them in a passionate prayer and with a further admonition brought the service to a close.

Meiling and her mother sat quietly for a few moments, stunned by the arrest of Pastor Yang. The congregation had begun to move slowly toward the door in absolute silence as each contemplated what all this meant.

Meiling leaned close to her mother and whispered, "We must not be afraid; only trust in the Lord who is our helper."

Mrs. Woo brushed the tears from her eyes as she grasped her daughter's hand. "I will try," she said, "but your father's warnings are beginning to come true. Oh, when will it touch our home?" she added as her shoulders shook with deep sobs.

A hand rested on Mrs. Woo's shoulder. She looked up into the eyes of Mrs. Wen, also clouded with tears. "We have the sure promises of God to stand on," she said gently. "Jesus said that we would suffer, but that He would be with us in the midst of the trial. Now is the time for us to lean our full weight on Him."

The two women held each other tightly for a few moments with an understanding others could not yet comprehend. The hot breath of the dragon was breathing down their necks, but they stood triumphantly on the promises. Both smiled and promised to pray for each other.

Meiling and her mother walked home very slowly as they reviewed the happenings of the morning. As they entered their home, Mr. Woo met them at the door with ashen face and troubled look.

"A special news report just was aired stating that Pastor Yang had been arrested for breaking the law. Is that true?" he asked. "Oh, Father, it is true," replied Meiling as Mrs. Woo burst into tears. She told the whole sad story from beginning to end. Not one detail was left out. "And you say a policeman struck the old elder and pushed him back into his seat?" he asked incredulously.

"He was a young man, big and strong," Meiling responded. "The crack on his face could be heard all over the congregation," she said. "Everyone gasped at the treatment of our elder."

"I don't know what is happening to our country," cried Mrs. Woo. "But how could this be on the radio already?" asked Meiling. "It just happened less than an hour ago." "I suspect that every detail was planned and that the announcements were written long before the arrest was made," replied Mr. Woo. "But that is deception of the worst kind," said Meiling. "You're right, my daughter, but expect it from now on. The only thing that will be permitted is the will of the Communists." "Oh, Father, does this mean that you will be subjected to this same kind of treatment?"

"Daughter, we must be prepared for anything to happen. There is no telling how low the Communists will stoop to enforce their will on the people. It's a very sad day for China—a very sad day!"

Arriving at the police station, Pastor Yang was hustled inside and pushed into a holding cell with his hands still in handcuffs. The door slammed shut as he looked around the dimly lit room. It was bare, not a piece of furniture in the room. There was nothing else to do but squat on the floor and lean back against the wall. It was not very comfortable with his hands behind his back, but he needed some rest from the bruising punishment he had received. His face was swollen and throbbing from the blow received at the church and his lips were swollen from the blow in the van. He wondered what was to become of him.

About a half-hour later, he heard footsteps coming down the corridor, and a key being inserted into the lock. As the door swung open, he looked into the hard, steely eyes of a man who had already become accustomed to ordering prisoners around.

"Stand when a police officer enters the room," he rasped, "and show respect."

Pastor Yang struggled to his feet with great effort, his heart pounding. *Lord Jesus,* he prayed silently, *I need Your help now. Give me courage to stand this test and be faithful to you.*

"Take him to the interrogation room," the officer ordered a lower ranking policeman.

Taking hold of Pastor Yang's arm, the officer guided him down the hall to another stark room with a table and only one chair. Sitting at the table was the police chief who glared at Pastor Yang with hatred spilling out of his eyes.

"How dare you defy the People's Republic of China," he began with an ugly snarl. "You were told to submit your sermons to the authorities before delivering them to the people. On what grounds can you justify this defiance of orders?" he fairly shouted.

With strong voice, Pastor Yang replied politely, "Sir, I did not intentionally disobey orders. We were informed that the regulations would be given to us, and thus far, I have not received any instructions, nor has anyone informed me where I am to submit my manuscripts."

"Do not attempt to make excuses," the police chief glared. "The papers were delivered to the gatekeeper this morning at

10:15 A.M. See, here is his signature proving he received it," he replied triumphantly. "But sir, the papers could not be delivered to me personally because the service began at 10:00 A.M."

"The papers reached your church before you delivered your sermon," he responded irritably. "It is not my responsibility if your gatekeeper was negligent. The papers were at your church before you spoke, and therefore you have broken the law," he said with finality.

"But." began Pastor Yang, "that is unreasonable . . ."

"Quiet," shouted the police chief. "I will not tolerate your in-solence. Answer my questions without any excuses. Do you un-derstand?" he glared as he pounded the table. "Now tell me the names and addresses of the leaders of your church, and my secre-tary here will write them down."

Pastor Yang stood erect, but his heart was racing. He could not reveal names and addresses or those people would be arrested and interrogated as well.

"Sir, it is not possible to give you the names and addresses from memory," he replied as he stalled for time.

"How long have you been the pastor of this church?" he shouted.

"I have been here for ten years," he replied knowing that this answer would infuriate the police chief.

"Ten years," he screamed as he stood to his feet and came over and cuffed the pastor on the ear. "Ten years, and you do not know where the people live?" His face was livid with rage. "I will give you another chance to tell me who they are and where they live, and if you refuse, we have ways to make you willing," he said menacingly.

"I am sorry, sir. I could lead you to their homes, but I cannot tell you their addresses from memory," he answered quietly.

"Take him away," shouted the police chief to two officers who were summoned, "and bring back the information I want."

As they marched him down the stairs to a lower floor of the building, he knew that he was about to be beaten until he revealed the names of the elders. *"Jesus, You bore so much for me. Help me now to bear up under this beating and sustain me through this ordeal. May I never disgrace Your name and turn my back on You or Your people."*

He was delivered into the hands of three men with masks on their faces. They opened the handcuffs and faced him toward the wall, and then, pulling his arms upward, they locked them into a clamp attached to the wall. The change of position of his arms brought temporary relief to his aching arms, but he knew it would be short-lived.

"Now," spoke up one of the masked men, "will you give us the names and addresses of the elders of the church or must we persuade you to do so?"

"I cannot give you that information." replied Pastor Yang quietly.

With a loud thud, the lash of a whip struck his back, causing his knees to buckle and his full weight to pull savagely on his wrists. The blow had caught him by surprise, and he cried out in pain as he struggled to stand to his feet.

Lord Jesus, help me not to cry out. Help me to be strong for Your glory, he prayed.

"Are you ready to give us the information we want?" spoke up the policeman again.

"No, I am not able," he replied.

Lash upon lash of the whip stung his body through his clothes. The man paused and asked again, "How much longer will you refuse to give us the information? Give it to us now," he shouted as he punched him in the face.

Pastor Yang made no sound. Another blow to his head brought blood from his ear and a dull, throbbing sensation in his head. Still no answer, but his body slumped and hung from his hands. Mercifully, he had passed out.

They unshackled him and dragged his limp body up the stairs and dumped it on the floor of a cell. The door clanged shut as they went to report to the chief. Pastor Yang didn't know how long he lay there, but it must have been several hours. When he awakened, he looked around in the dim light of a twenty-five-watt bulb that would be all the light he would have night and day for weeks to come. He tried to move, but the pain was almost unbearable. As his eyes became accustomed to the dim light, he discovered that there was a bamboo bed in one corner, but no blankets. In the other corner was a toilet bucket and nothing else. The cold dampness of the stone floor had penetrated his whole body. *I must get to the bed, somehow,* he groaned as he struggled to get up. All he could do was crawl painfully to the bed, and with supreme effort, he pulled himself up onto the hard surface of the bed. He lay there exhausted. *Thank You, Jesus,* he sighed, for *helping me. I did not reveal any names, and I did not cry out a second time,* he said with joy as he realized that he had passed the first test.

He lifted his left arm painfully to look at his watch to see what time it was. It had been removed. In the semi-darkness of his windowless cell it was impossible to know whether it was day or night, another tactic of his persecutors to confuse him and make him talk. Suddenly, as he lay there with throbbing back and face, the room seemed to be lit by a soft and glorious glow. *"Don't be afraid, My child,"* spoke a soothing voice in his heart. *"I have many people to bring to salvation through your testimony. I am with you in all of these trials and sufferings. Only be strong and courageous. I will never leave you."*

The glow faded as he realized his precious Lord had spoken to him in this miserable cell. Then he realized the pain in his body and face had subsided. He sat up and looked around in wonder as the thrill of the presence of Jesus filled his heart. "Jesus is with me," he spoke out loud. "He touched me! He came to visit me here in this cell," he exclaimed with joy. "Oh, thank You, Jesus. Thank You for the new strength You have given me. Thank You for Your promises that will sustain me. Oh, thank You, my Jesus. I will never turn back."

The cold dampness of the cell did not matter. A glorious warmth flooded his soul and his body was relieved and warmed. He lay there praising God until he fell asleep.

He was awakened by the scraping sound of a small opening in the door of his cell. A man peered in and called out that some food would be pushed through a slot at the bottom of the door. Pastor Yang slowly got to his feet and moved toward the door. A tin bowl was pushed in containing a weak rice gruel. With some effort he bent over and picked up the bowl, and walked slowly back to his bed. He sat down and gave thanks for this provision of food. Since no spoon was provided, he raised the bowl to his swollen lips and drank slowly, relishing the refreshing taste. It had been almost twenty-four hours since he had last eaten or had a drink of water. He made it last as long as possible and drained every drop from the bowl.

The first thing in the morning, Mrs. Yang went to the police station with a thermos bottle of hot tea. She was turned away by the officer at the door who also refused to accept the thermos.

"You will be informed when your husband can receive the things you bring him," he said simply. "Now return to your home, and don't come again," he said firmly.

"Please," she begged, "just give him this thermos of hot tea."

"The People's Government of China will provide all he needs. Now leave," he said curtly with a menacing gesture. She realized it was futile to continue, but as she walked slowly down the steps, she decided to circle the block on which the police station was located and pray for her husband. She would do that many times in the next weeks, walking slowly around the block, and praying that God would sustain her husband and lighten the ordeal he was passing through. Several weeks later when he was released, he would testify that it was the prayers of his wife and those of his congregation that sustained him during those horrible days.

How many days he spent in the semi-darkness of his dingy, smelly cell where neither time of day or night could be determined, he did not know. There was only one brief encounter with a human being and that was when the slot on the floor was opened and the bowl of food and drink was pushed in. The empty bowl remained on the floor by the slot until the next meal, which meant that the cockroaches that infested the place also worked the bowl over very thoroughly. In the dim light of the cell, he watched the roaches scurry all around the bowl. He wondered if it was ever washed before the next meal! He wondered, too, when his next meeting with the police chief would take place.

He prepared himself by quoting the long passages of Scripture he had memorized. How glad he was that he had encouraged his people to memorize the Word. He had no idea how many hours passed as he lay on his hard bamboo bed reveling in the rich treasures of God's Word. Sometimes he burst into singing as joy filled his heart, and he remembered how much Jesus suffered to save him from sin. Still, it was difficult in the semi-darkness with nothing to do and nothing to read. Satan came and reminded him of his comfortable home and his family. He whispered in his ear that it was very foolish to take this road of suffering. *Why not give the chief the names he wants. He will find them out anyway,* Satan whispered at times, while at other times he fairly shouted these thoughts in his ears. It was then he turned to Scripture as Jesus did in the wilderness, and quoted it to his adversary. Satan left at the sound of God's powerful Word. In those moments, the wonderful peace of God flooded his heart, and he quietly rejoiced as he worshipped the Lord.

Then began daily visits to the chief's office, and always the same questions were asked. As Pastor Yang continued to withhold the names of his elders; many blows were administered to his head and body by the young guards who always stood at attention waiting for orders. Day after day he was returned to his cellblock, beaten, weary, hungry and thirsty, but always the glow of the Lord filled his heart and gave him new strength. Three weeks slipped slowly by as his body became weaker and weaker.

One morning while quoting Psalm 27 and reveling in the truth that the Lord was his light and salvation, and that he need not be afraid of anyone, he heard the familiar scratching sound of a key in the lock. Moving slowly to a sitting position, he waited expectantly.

The door swung open and two guards entered. Commanding him to stand, they placed the handcuffs on him again and led him away. He moved slowly since his body still ached from his many beatings. Each time he entered the brilliantly lit room where the chief always sat behind the table, the lights pained his eyes after hours in semi-darkness in his cell. He blinked several times to relieve the pain and focus his attention on the chief who said in a civil voice, "Now, Yang, are you ready to give me the names and addresses of the elders of your church? You see, I am a good man, and I do not wish to cause you any pain, but I must have those names. It will be to your advantage to give them to me quickly so that I can set you free to go home to your family. You would like that, wouldn't you? Your wife is missing you, too. We have observed her walking around this police station every day so I know she is waiting for you to come home. Now, let's be sensible. Give me the names and you can go home."

At that moment, Pastor Yang sensed the awesome presence of the Holy Spirit flooding his heart. Courage surged through him as he realized that he was not alone. Jesus was right there in the room with him. He stood erect and looked the chief squarely in the eye.

"Sir," he began with a strong voice, "you are asking me to do something that is foreign to Chinese people. You are asking me to condemn my neighbors, to reveal confidential matters between loyal friends. As a good Chinese, would you do that to your friends?"

The chief's eyes flickered for a moment at the impact of the question. He recovered quickly and responded. "Yang, listen to me. We are no longer talking about the old feudal Chinese system and protocol. This is the New China, and we are now the People's Republic of China, a Communist state that is working to protect the workers and bring in the paradise the imperialists have denied us. You will provide me the names and addresses immediately or you will be sent back for more re-education."

The chief's face had drained of all color, and it seemed to Pastor Yang that the man was trembling slightly. His question had struck a chord in the man's heart even though he was desperately attempting to cover it up. A wave of pity filled his heart as he watched this man with almost unlimited power tremble before the truth.

"Sir," he began again, "I will always be a loyal Chinese no matter what political group controls our government. I will make every legitimate effort to support our government, but I cannot comply with your request. It goes against everything Chinese, and also my Christian faith."

With that the chief moved from behind his desk and walked over to him.

"Who gave you the right to lecture me, the representative of the People's Republic?" he shouted as he struck him across his face with the back of his hand. "Answer me, now, with the information I want." He struck him again bringing blood from his nose that was still tender from earlier beatings.

"I would be denying Jesus if I did that," he responded courageously, "and I cannot do that."

"Then, I will teach you the new doctrine of Communism," he said as he flailed at his face with repeated blows. "Take him away," he ordered, "and get the information I want."

A guard grabbed his arm, swung him around sharply, and shoved him down the stairs to his dark cell.

Chapter 10

WILL IT NEVER STOP?

Pastor Yang was led down the hallway to the lower dungeon where he had experienced his first beating. He shuddered as he walked along slowly as the guard prodded him with an electric stick.

Lord Jesus, he prayed silently, *they are going to beat me again. Help me to endure this suffering for Your name's sake, and help me to resist to the end. I will not divulge any information to these cruel men, but I need Your help. I thank You that I am counted worthy to drink the cup of Your suffering. Help me to bring glory to Your name and salvation to these my persecutors.*

Reaching the lowest level of the prison, Pastor Yang sensed that this would be his worst treatment thus far. The rank odor of urine filled the dark chamber where countless victims had been tortured. A moment of fear gripped his heart as the guard roughly placed handcuffs on his wrists and ordered him to bend over and touch his feet. Clamping handcuffs on his ankles, the guard proceeded to link the two sets of handcuffs. Attaching a rope dangling from the ceiling to the coupled handcuffs, he stepped back as the head guard took over.

"Yang," the guard shouted loudly, "I give you one more chance to divulge the names of the elders of your church, or I will be forced to get them another way. Tell me the names of the elders," he commanded harshly. "Now!"

From his bent over position, Pastor Yang spoke softly, but firmly as he said, "I am a follower of Jesus Christ. He is my Lord and my Savior. I will never deny Him or bring disgrace to His holy name."

"Yang," interrupted the guard, "stop this ridiculous stuff about Jesus. You are about to get the beating of your life. I don't want to hurt you. My mother attends your church, and she would not want you to be hurt. Please, give me the names," he pleaded with a softening tone in his voice. "Be reasonable, man, be reasonable."

"Dear brother," he answered, "my heart is filled with pity and sorrow for you. You can only hurt my body, but you can never touch my soul. I will not desert my Lord, and neither will my wife."

With a fierce angry scream, the guard ordered his henchmen to hoist Pastor Yang from his hands and feet. The two men jerked the rope sharply, and as it tightened in the pulley in the ceiling, Pastor Yang was yanked off his feet. He landed heavily on his back as his arms and legs were pulled taut. As the men pulled the second time, he was hoisted from the floor and suspended in mid-air. A third jerk again pulled every muscle in his body and stretched them to the limit causing searing pain to shoot through every part of his body. Hanging upside down and swinging in space, the blood rushed to his head and left him faint and dizzy.

Faintly he heard the guard's voice, "Yang, give me those names."

He gritted his teeth to keep from screaming. "My God," he gasped, "help me now."

With a resounding whack a bamboo pole landed on the calf of his legs. The excruciating pain ripped through his body. "Oh, my God," he groaned. "Help me to sing Your praises."

To the surprise of the guards standing around, this incredible man began to sing! They stood there in amazement, not knowing what to do.

He sang in a croaky voice as the tears flowed from his eyes, "My Jesus . . . I love thee . . . I know thou art mine . . . For thee all the follies of sin I resign." His voice grew stronger and filled the room as the guards stood silently by, awestruck by what they were witnessing. "If ever I love thee," he gasped, ". . . My Jesus . . . 'tis now," he ended triumphantly.

Recovering from the shock of a man singing while hanging upside down by his hands and feet, the guard administered more blows. Pastor Yang lost consciousness as he swung helplessly.

"Take him down and take him back to his cell," ordered the guard with resignation. "We'll get no information from him now."

The two young guards lowered his body to the floor, and picking him up by arms and feet, they half-carried, half-dragged him to his cell. Soft groans came from Pastor Yang as he revived slightly, but he soon lapsed into unconsciousness again. The next day when the guard reported to his superiors that the prisoner had not touched his food and was unresponsive, the prison doctor was ordered to examine him.

Taking one look at Pastor Yang, he ordered him moved to the hospital infirmary. It was several days before he opened his eyes and looked around the room.

"Where am I?" he asked weakly of the nurse standing near by.

"In the prison hospital," she responded. "Would you like something to drink?

"Yes, please," he responded through parched lips. "Oh," he groaned as he tried to move his arm, "I can't hold the glass."

She spooned some water into his mouth as he floated off into unconsciousness again. The doctor stopped by a little later and asked, "Has he come to, yet?"

"For a few moments."

Looking at him, the doctor replied, "Give him food and water whenever possible. We must get him out of here before he dies," he said matter-of-factly. He reported immediately to the chief, "If we don't release him now, he will die on our hands. Bring him back in later when he recovers, but don't let him die here. Someone might use it against us some day."

"You're right," he responded. "His wife walks by here every day. I'll release him to her immediately,"

A couple of hours later, as Mrs. Yang walked by on her daily prayer walk, a young policeman stepped out and called to her.

"Mrs. Yang, the chief requests that you come in and take your husband home," he said simply.

"Take my husband home?" she cried excitedly. "Oh. Praise the Lord."

She followed the young man into the station and was told to wait for the chief. A half-hour passed before he made his appearance.

"Mrs. Yang," he began, "your husband has not cooperated at all, but right now he is not well, and we have decided that it would be better for him to return home. Later, we will ask him to come in again. The doctor is getting your husband ready to leave. Go get a rickshaw and take him home."

"What is wrong with my husband?" she asked fearing that his heart was giving him trouble.

"I think he must have fallen and hurt his head," the chief lied, averting her eyes. "But he will recover in a few days, I am sure. Now go and get a rickshaw."

Her heart was pounding with excitement and joy, but also apprehension. Something about the chief's comments didn't seem to ring true. Rushing out to hire a rickshaw, she wondered what the true facts were. Flagging down a rickshaw, she said, "Wait here, please. My husband is being released because he is ill," she said innocently.

"Probably beaten up so he can't walk," said the rickshaw puller matter-of-factly. "I've been here before."

"Really?" Mrs. Yang gasped. She didn't have time to say more because the door to the police station opened and two men came out carrying a man whose head was bandaged. *Could this be my husband,* she thought as she rushed over to help settle him in the rickshaw. "Chiwah," she said tenderly, tears running down her cheeks. "Is it really you? Oh, what have they done to you?" she cried. He didn't respond; he only groaned and lay there lifelessly.

"Let's go," she said to the puller. "Try and avoid any rough places in the road. I think he is badly injured."

"Beaten," said the man with disgust. "They are monsters."

As they turned into the church compound, she called to some men nearby to come and help carry her husband into the house. Word spread quickly that Pastor Yang had been released and was badly injured. In just a few minutes, a large crowd of believers had gathered to pray for their beloved pastor. A Christian nurse returning home from the hospital took charge.

"We must get these filthy clothes off and these wounds cleansed," she said. "Bring me warm water and call a doctor," she ordered. "Oh, poor pastor," she wept as she removed the bandages from his head. "He has been brutally beaten. Some of these wounds are days old," she observed, "but many are fresh wounds. What kind of people would do this to anyone, let alone a pastor?" she asked as she gently cleansed his wounds.

"Chiwah," Mrs. Yang called softly, "can you hear me?"

But there was no response.

A doctor friend rushed in some time later, and after examining him, he announced, "He has been brutally beaten with a whip and probably a bamboo pole. There are no broken bones, but I suspect he has suffered internal injuries. He must be moved to the hospital immediately."

Meiling opened the door to her home and rushed into her mother's arms. "Mother," she cried, "Pastor Yang has been released from prison, and he has been badly beaten. He is unconscious. Mrs. Yang has taken him to the hospital," she sobbed as her mother held her close.

"Meiling," she spoke soothingly to her daughter, "sit down and tell me what this is all about."

Between sobs that shook her whole body, she told her everything she knew.

"Oh, Mother, I'm so frightened for Father," she wept. "If they treat a pastor like this, they will not spare a school principal," she sobbed. "Oh, Mother, what's going to happen to Father?"

"I don't know, Meiling, but Pastor Yang has been teaching us if we intend to follow Jesus, we must take up our cross every day and follow Him, and when we do, we can lean our full weight on Him. I only wish your father would make his own personal decision before it is too late."

The news of Pastor Yang's treatment reached Mr. Woo at school.

"It is unbelievable that the Communists would have the arrogance to beat Pastor Yang so savagely," he said when he returned home. "No one will be safe from such dreadful interrogations," he continued.

"We must face each day through the strength of the Lord," replied Mrs. Woo.

"I am still searching for the truth," he admitted as he looked at Meiling and then at his wife. "I know you are praying for me. Keep it up. I am getting closer."

Everyone was shocked when a political officer was assigned to Mr. Woo's school. On his very first day on the job, he ordered a weekly teacher's indoctrination session, and in this very first session, he announced in a somber voice that each week everyone would be required to be present including the principal. The announcement caught Mr. Woo by surprise, and he wondered why he was singled out in this way. They were also informed that they would be expected to criticize the school administrators and one another in their reports because it was through such criticism that they could throw off the evil past and make progress in the New China. Silence reigned as they filed out quietly, wondering what they would write in their report, but more fearful of what others would write about them! The Communists were winning the battle for people's minds and allegiance.

Mr. Woo made his way along the deserted street, making certain to stay in the shadows whenever possible. In lighted areas he paused, looking in all directions before hurrying across to the next shadow. He reached Pastor Yang's home at the church and knocked cautiously as his eyes constantly swept the area for any signs of danger. The door opened a crack as the gatekeeper inquired who was there in a soft whisper.

"I'm Principal Woo from the high school, Meiling's father. I would like to visit Pastor Yang. It is very important."

"Ah, Meiling's father," repeated the gatekeeper, "come inside quickly. I will see if Pastor Yang can see you. Please wait here a moment."

In a few moments, Mrs. Yang hurried back to the gate to greet Mr. Woo and invite him in.

"My husband will be delighted to see you," she said warmly. "He has been resting today and is feeling much better," she added as she led the way into their living room.

"I am so glad to see you, Mr. Woo," Pastor Yang said as he rose slowly to greet the principal. "I am still moving rather slowly," he admitted with a smile. "My body is not as young as it used to be, and it is healing more slowly than I would like, but I praise God that I am experiencing His wonderful healing day by day."

"Pardon this intrusion on your time this evening, Pastor," he began. "I know all about you through my daughter, Meiling, and my wife who attend here regularly."

"And I know all about you," he responded. "We have been praying for you."

"Your prayers and those of my family are working," he said simply with a slight smile on his face. "I have been searching for God ever since Meiling started coming to your church with Anching. I was so impressed by their faith and the peace they found. Meiling gave me the Gospel of John, and then, I was so fascinated by it that I went and bought a New Testament, and I've been reading it every day."

"That's wonderful news, Mr. Woo," he replied joyfully. "I want you to know it really pays to follow Jesus no matter what happens in life. You see, eternal life in heaven is the only thing that counts."

"I am beginning to feel that way, too, and that is the reason I have come to see you tonight. I have heard of the terrible beatings you endured at the hands of the police for your faith, and yet you have not turned back."

"Oh, Brother Woo, let me assure you that Jesus is more precious than life itself. The beatings are temporary, but Jesus is forever. I will never turn my back on Him."

"Pastor Yang, I am sure the Communists will soon call me in for questioning, and who knows what else. I may be facing death in the next few weeks, but I am not ready, like you, to meet God. Can you help me?"

For the next hour, Pastor Yang led Mr. Woo through the steps of receiving the Lord. As Mr. Woo finished praying, his face lit up with a relieved smile as he grasped the pastor's hand.

"I am a child of God at last," he said over and over again. "I have been seeking for so long to find the answer. Now I feel able to face the trials of the future. Meiling has helped me so much, and assured me that Jesus would go with me, anywhere—even to death. Your experiences have encouraged me to come tonight, and now I will trust the Lord for the future."

"Mr. Woo, you will never regret this decision. It is the best one you have ever made," he said with a warm smile. After praying together, Mr. Woo slipped out into the night again, only now his heart was light as God smiled upon him.

Things began to fall apart very quickly for Mr. Woo at the school with the appointment of Comrade Ming, the political boss for the school. His first action was to humiliate Mrs. Ma, the much-loved and long-time vice principal. Using the new Communist tactics of a "struggle meeting," he succeeded in demoting her to the lowest level in the school—a dishwasher in the kitchen. Fear gripped the hearts of every teacher as they watched the heartless demotion take place publicly before them all.

Comrade Ming made use of a former teacher, Miss Tang, who had been dismissed from the school five years ago. What he did not allow to be entered as testimony during Mrs. Ma's trial was the fact that she had been dismissed for stealing school supplies. In a reversal of justice, she was reinstated, only this time as the new vice principal simply by the decision of Comrade Ming, but certainly not on her merits as a school administrator.

Three difficult weeks passed for Mr. Woo. Miss Tang's primary function was to serve as a mole in the school. Each day she reported directly to Ming all the scuttlebutt she could dig up. Everyone was aware of her spying and hated her for it, but everyone knew it was futile to object.

The sword finally fell one Monday morning for Mr. Woo as he entered his office. There, waiting for him with an official looking envelope in her hand, was Miss Tang.

"Comrade Ming requested me to deliver this letter to you in person, and have you sign that you have received it," she said with a smug look on her face.

"His office is less than fifty feet from mine. Could he not deliver this letter himself?"

"I am only doing what I was instructed to do," she replied impudently. "Now, please sign right here," she insisted.

No sense in making any further scene, he thought. *I know what is in the letter anyway, so get it over with,* he reasoned to himself.

Taking the paper, he signed his name. Miss Tang smiled triumphantly and left the office.

He sat at his desk, envelope in hand, turning it over and over without opening it. He dreaded opening it for he knew it was a summons to an accusation meeting. His worst fears had come to pass.

Lord Jesus, my new Lord and Savior, he prayed silently as he held the letter firmly in his trembling hands, *when I took the step by faith to receive You as my Lord and Savior, I understood I was taking up my cross to follow You. The test has come. Help me to be strong in spite of everything that is about to take place, and help me to bring glory to Your name. Amen.*

A sense of awe enveloped him as he began to open the letter. Instead of fear, there was peace. Instead of anger at Comrade Ming for his deceitfulness, there was forgiveness. Instead of despair, there was the sense of the presence of the Lord undergirding him. It was strange because never before when facing such a difficult situation had he ever been able to look death in the eye so calmly.

This is what You promised would happen, dear Lord, he prayed. *You have called on me to give testimony to Your great power, and with Your help, I will not fail.*

Unfolding the letter with impressive seals from the local Communist authorities, he read, *Mr. Woo Mingtao, you are hereby summoned to appear before faculty, staff and student body on 16 February 1953 to answer the charge of incompetence and dereliction of duties as principal of the Puyang High School. Failure to appear will constitute admission of the crimes you are accused of by reliable witnesses of the school.* Signed Ming Fanling, Political Officer, and Colonel Ching Fukang, Military Attaché for the People's Republic of China, Wuchang, Hubei Province.

So they are rolling out the highest political officer of the region, he thought. *At least I will not be subject to the whims of Ming,* he reasoned. *Not that it makes any difference. The case against me is already decided. They will simply pretend this is a trial in order to make a fool out of me. In the end, I will be relieved of my role here as principal,* he thought as he laid the envelope on the table and buried his face in his hands. His shoulders heaved with a big sob as hot tears coursed down his cheeks. Lifting his head, he looked at the calendar through his tears. *One more week,* he thought, *and my life will be changed forever.*

Walking slowly home, he paused at the little park and watched the spotted doves pecking at the ground in search of food. *What was it I read the other day in Matthew's gospel?* he tried to recall. *Something about the little sparrows being fed by a loving God. Yes, that was it. It went something like "Your heavenly Father feeds the sparrows! And you are worth more to Him than many sparrows." Think of that,* he mused as he watched the doves pecking. *And then,* he thought, *Jesus said something like "Don't worry about anything. Seek first the kingdom of God, and everything else will be given to you." I must read that again,* he thought as he continued to gaze at the doves. *I'm worth more to Jesus than many doves, and He will take care of my family and me.*

He quickened his steps, and by the time he reached home, he was prepared to break the news to his family and lead them quietly in prayer.

"What will you be accused of?" his wife asked anxiously. "You have treated everyone fairly, and you have never cheated the government of taxes," she said as she wiped the tears from her eyes.

"Now is the time we trust the Lord," he said tenderly to his wife. "It is going to be bad, and very humiliating, but I will not be standing there alone like I would have a few weeks ago."

He told the family about the doves he had seen on the way home and the passage in Matthew. "No matter what we are called upon to bear," he continued, "I now know that Jesus will be there to help us through it all just as Meiling has been saying."

His family huddled around him in silence, taking strength from this man who only a few weeks before was struggling with the issues of faith. They were buoyed by his faith, the youngest believer among them, but one who had come to Christ by a long road of doubts and fears. Now that it was settled, he could be strong and give to his family the courage they needed.

For the next several days, he secluded himself in his office. No one dared to approach him anyway lest they be accused of supporting him. Long-time teacher friends passed him in silence and with downcast eyes. The week passed slowly until the dreaded night arrived.

"Just pray that no matter what happens, I will be faithful and a good witness," he said as he left home with his wife.

The hall was crowded for this command performance. Long-time friends cautiously dabbed at their eyes as sorrow got the best of them. Only a few carefully planted Communist sympathizers attempted to carry on an animated conversation, parroting the party line about loyalty to Chairman Mao and the government. Every head moved ever so slightly as Mr. and Mrs. Woo entered the hall and took their places on the front row. Meiling sat with a large group of alumni, now students at the university, who were instructed to appear as a group. She sensed the purpose was to embarrass her family and perhaps single her out for future accusations. None of her former friends seated with her spoke to her. All sat in stony silence afraid even to look in her direction. She glanced over at her parents. They sat erect and unashamed, knowing full well that this was going to be a terrible night they would always remember, but they showed no fear for they had all committed themselves to the Lord before they left home. Mrs. Woo reminded her husband that Pastor Yang had spoken about being brought before magistrates and kings, but in that moment, the Holy Spirit gave them the words to say.

A side door opened and an announcer ordered the people to stand as the officials entered. Colonel Ching Fukang led the way to the platform followed by the political boss, Ming, who glanced triumphantly at the crowded auditorium, and then at Mr. Woo standing with head erect looking straight ahead. He gloated as he sensed victory within his grasp and knew his power over this crowd was on the rise. He loved every minute of it and was determined to make the most of this trial.

The colonel called the meeting to order and requested a secretary to read the charges. Up until now, Mr. Woo did not know the details of what he was charged with. He listened intently.

The secretary cleared her throat and began. "Woo Mingtao, principal of Puyang High School for the past twenty-eight years, is hereby charged with incompetence in handling the affairs of the school as evidenced by the dismissal of the talented Miss Tang Liensu five years ago. She has been reinstated as a staff member of the school and recently promoted to assistant principal. Miss Tang will testify that she was humiliated before the entire school staff by her dismissal, and that she suffered irreparable psychological damage by the wrongful actions of Woo."

What a travesty of justice! his heart screamed as he listened. *This Tang woman was found guilty of stealing. She has been hand picked to bring condemnation on Mrs. Ma and now on me,* he thought as his throat tightened with tension. He licked his dry lips as he realized the case was stacked against him. *Oh God,* he prayed silently, *help my dear wife to bear up under this injustice.* He glanced in her direction without moving his head and noticed her vigorously twisting her handkerchief. His thoughts were interrupted as the secretary read on.

"Secondly, Woo is charged with accepting a bribe by the deposed, and now deceased capitalist, Pang Muching, who paid Woo the sum of 10,000 yuan to insure that his son, Pang Luping, would represent Puyang High School at the fall festival. This constitutes unlawful suppression of ordinary citizens like Wen Anching who was deprived of his right to represent the school by virtue of his superior essay he had entered in the contest. Woo is further charged with complicity to defraud the government by his association with Pang Muching, who was condemned and punished for his crime of bribery and association with an army officer of the now defunct Nationalist government."

Remorse gripped Mr. Woo's heart as the sad events of the Fall Festival Contest were entered as testimony against him. *Yes, he was guilty of giving in to Pang's pressure on the contest, but not of accepting the bribe personally. I will defend myself against that charge,* he decided as emotion gripped his heart. *Could this be an attempt to get at Meiling?* he wondered as the whole sad story of Anching flashed through his mind. *These Communists are so subtle,* he thought. *They start a case against someone long before their accusation begins.* Confusing thoughts raced through his mind. *I must be careful when I speak, as my words will be used against my family at another time.* The secretary read on in a monotone.

"Thirdly, following the imperialist teachings of the United States," the secretary read in an unemotional tone of voice that did not reveal the seriousness of the so-called crimes he was being charged with, "he has become a Christian in opposition to the teachings of our great leader, Chairman Mao Zedong."

She paused for effect as a slight gasp rippled through the audience. Everyone was well aware by now that the new government looked with disdain on Christians. If one wanted to gain popularity with the government or leaders of the area political groups, it was advantageous to bring this accusation against anyone on trial.

"Evidence of his defection from the accepted party doctrine will be supplied by Miss Tang in her testimony."

Closing her folder, she handed it to the colonel who scowled menacingly at Mr. Woo. Rising to his feet, he stated in harsh tones, "The defendant will take the stand to answer these serious charges against the People's Republic of China. Witnesses will verify these serious actions by the defendant. You, the assembled members of the faculty, staff and alumni, and friends of the People's Republic of China will be called upon to issue the verdict upon such vermin as Woo who has polluted our great land."

In saying these words, he showed his hand. Mr. Woo's heart sank as he realized that the trial was rigged for political reasons, and there was no hope for him.

Oh, Lord, he prayed again, *give me courage to stand this test.* His prayer was interrupted as he heard the colonel calling on Comrade Ming, the prosecutor, to begin the case.

"Mr. Prosecutor," he said as he turned to Ming, "are you ready to proceed with the trial?"

"I am, your honor," he replied with a smirk on his face as he looked toward Mr. Woo. "Will the defendant take the stand and only give us truthful answers to our questions."

Mr. Woo stood with sinking heart knowing it would be futile to try and defend himself. Meiling watched with a deep sense of sorrow as her father took the stand. His eyes were without their usual warmth and sparkle, but his head was high and strong. *The tone of the proceedings is not in his favor,* she thought, but she was encouraged that his demeanor spoke of strength and character. She shot a prayer heavenward for the superhuman strength her father needed now.

Ming looked with triumph on his hapless victim as he said, "Your honor, I will prove that the defendant has shown favoritism in the administration of the school; that he has accepted bribes to enrich himself; and that he has committed the unacceptable crime of giving aid to the imperialists by following their religious views. This is contrary to the expressed declarations of our supreme leader Chairman Mao Zedong. The case of Miss Tang's improper dismissal is already known to the court and by the conviction of Mrs. Ma, the former inept assistant principal, the defendant is found guilty as he was the perpetrator of the whole case."

Miss Tang's testimony consumed fifteen minutes, but in light of Mrs. Ma's conviction, Mr. Woo was like a mouse in the paws of a big cat determined to eventually kill it. The second charge of bribery was not as easy for Ming as Mr. Woo was able to name dozens of people on the faculty and staff who benefited by Mr. Pang's annual contributions. He was stung by Ming's insistence that Anching, from the peasant class, had been deprived of the prize by the rich man's son. In the end, Ming prevailed.

Meiling stiffened at the sound of Anching's name, but she dared not allow any change on her face. Too many people were watching for some reaction, as that would provide a cause for a future accusation. But the sword was stabbing deep in her heart. It had been three years since she had had any word from him. *Where was he? Was he alive or dead?* How her heart ached for some word from him. Sitting motionless, and staring straight ahead, one would not have known the pain of the sword that pierced her heart.

As the trial proceeded, Mr. Woo was shocked at the extent of the cruel attack on his integrity and Christian faith.

"Isn't it true, Miss Tang," he began as she took the stand a second time, "that you discovered a Bible hidden in Woo's desk?"

"That is correct, Comrade Ming," she said accusingly. "On one occasion as I entered his office to give him a message from you, I saw him hastily put a black-colored book into his desk drawer and close it quickly."

"And how do you know it was a Bible, Miss Tang?" prodded Ming.

"Since our great leader, Chairman Mao, has instructed us to be very watchful of deceitful people like the defendant, I returned to the defendant's office after he had left, and searched the drawer. I immediately reported that to you so that the children of our school would not be poisoned by the imperialist teaching of this foreign book."

"Miss Tang," Ming beamed, "you are to be commended for your faithfulness in following our great leader's instructions. Without such vigilance, our great leader will be unable to uproot these dangerous ideas that have infiltrated our great country."

Meiling squirmed in her seat as anger surged through her body.

How can he commend her for invading her father's privacy? That is the height of deceit and improper behavior, she fairly screamed out in protest.

"Was there any other behavior that you observed in the defendant that proves he is a believer in this foreign religion?"

"Oh, yes," she responded quickly. "On many occasions, I observed him closing his eyes and moving his lips. He was praying!" she said with venom in her voice. "Imagine, the principal of our school propagating this foreign religion of the imperialists!"

"Did you ever hear him praying out loud?" Ming asked triumphantly.

"No, I cannot say I did," she answered truthfully, "but I am acquainted with Christians, and I have observed that they all follow this same style."

"Do you know of any Christians in this audience?" asked Ming suddenly as if he were following through with a one-two punch.

Every eye was riveted on Miss Tang as tension mounted quickly. Ming was quick to observe the effect of his question and followed through immediately by demanding that she answer the question and name the people she knew who were Christians. A stony silence enveloped the audience, and those who were Christians in the group trembled at the implication of the question.

Miss Tang looked over the audience rather quickly, and then deliberately pointed to Mrs. Woo and said, "It has been reported to me by faithful followers of our great leader that Mrs. Woo frequently attends the church of Pastor Yang."

"Thank you, Miss Tang, for this important information. And is there anyone else here who deviates from our leader's instructions?"

Turning toward Meiling without a moment's hesitation, she pointed directly at her and replied, "Yes, Woo's daughter, Meiling, is a known Christian. While she was a student at the high school, she was an avowed Christian. She constantly sought to influence others to believe, and encouraged them to attend the church. What was especially bad about that was the fact that as the principal's daughter, she exercised unusual power over students who were afraid to resist her lest they be penalized by her father."

"Thank you, thank you, Miss Tang," answered Ming with a triumphant look in his eyes. "You may step down from the witness stand."

Meiling struggled to keep her composure while Mrs. Woo was terrified that Meiling had been dragged into the trial. Meiling's alumni friends dropped their eyes in shocked surprise at this turn of events. They felt uncomfortable sitting so close to her even though they knew the charge was not true. In all of these struggle meetings, the purpose was obvious—turn each one against the other. Make them afraid to speak out in protest, demand uniformity at the price of personal friendship and loyalty. Mr. Woo felt the pain of being stabbed in the back, not because Miss Tang had been snooping in his office, but because his beloved daughter was now implicated along with him.

"You have heard Miss Tang's testimony," he said as he directed his remarks to Mr. Woo. "What do you have to say about such behavior?"

As he stood there, he was reminded of Peter and John who were questioned by the authorities after the healing of the lame man at the beautiful gate of the temple. *Help me, Lord,* he prayed silently, *and give me the right words to say.*

"First of all," began Mr. Woo in a strong voice, "I have been wrongfully portrayed on each of the charges. The people of this audience have known me for many years, and they are acquainted with the fact that I have never personally profited by any gifts the school has received. Only the faculty and staff have profited by the higher salaries the school was able to give them."

Ming started to speak, but the colonel motioned for him to be quiet.

"Proceed," he ordered.

"If I were permitted to call witnesses for my side, and if they were permitted to give fair testimony without fear of reprisal, there would be dozens and dozens of people in this room who would testify that I have been a fair and just administrator of the school for these many years."

Ming stirred slightly, but he kept quiet.

Encouraged, Mr. Woo continued. "Now concerning the Bible that Miss Tang found in my desk after improperly searching my desk like a thief."

Ming jumped to his feet, interrupting hotly, "I object, your honor. The defendant has impinged the character of the state's witness, and I request that this testimony be expunged from the record."

"Mr. Woo," the Colonel responded coldly, "you will heed the warning of the prosecutor and refrain from expressing unfounded allegations of the state's witness. Now proceed with your testimony."

Unshaken by this rebuff, Mr. Woo continued.

"It is true that I had a Bible in my desk, and that I read it frequently. It brought me deep inner peace as I read the words of Jesus that everyone should love one another, even those who were unkind to you or sought to destroy you."

The audience again sat forward listening attentively. They were stunned that Mr. Woo admitted to reading the Bible, the forbidden book, now that the Communists had taken over. They were asking themselves, *Doesn't he know that it is forbidden to read the Bible?*

"As I read," he continued, "I discovered that Jesus offered everyone eternal life in heaven to all who believed in him. One day, after months of searching our Chinese classics, and reading about Chinese religions, I finally concluded that I needed Jesus Christ to be my Savior, and so I prayed to receive Him into my life. In that moment," he added quickly lest he be interrupted, "I discovered a most wonderful peace in my life such as I had never experienced before. I knew that I was now a child of God and bound for heaven."

"Enough," shouted the Colonel. "You may not use this witness stand to propagate the foreign religion of Christianity that our great leader, Chairman Mao has banned from our land."

Ming jumped to his feet, sensing that his opportunity had come.

"Your honor, the defendant has defiled the court room with this poisonous teaching of the imperialists. Therefore, I request that the defendant be ordered to sit on this high stool and that a dunce hat be placed on his head indicating that this court will not tolerate the foolish ideas of the imperialists."

As he said that, he reached under the table that was skirted with a cloth, and pulled out a twenty-four-inch tall dunce cap with the word "dunce" written on it. It was obvious to all that it had been prepared in advance and ready for this moment.

The colonel nodded in agreement as Ming ceremoniously placed the high stool in the middle of the platform and placed the hat on Mr. Woo's head. He hung a sign on his chest with the words, "Imperialist Dunce." Some sparse clapping erupted throughout the audience, but most hung their heads in shame as they witnessed the degrading of a beloved friend.

"And so you admit that you are a Christian, and you read the foreign book against the express orders of our great leader," Ming asked sarcastically. "Is that true?"

Mr. Woo fearlessly looked straight into the eyes of Mr. Ming and replied, "Comrade Ming, it is true. I am a Christian, and I believe that Jesus Christ is my Savior, and that He has given me eternal life. I am a witness for Jesus Christ."

"You are more of a dunce than I thought," he shouted hoarsely. "Don't you realize that this court has the power to punish you for beliefs that work against the People's Republic?"

"Yes," Mr. Woo responded slowly, "I am aware of that, but I love Jesus, and I can do nothing less than take my stand for Him. I am a loyal Chinese, and I will defend my country, but first I am a Christian."

Meiling watched her father with admiration glowing in her eyes. She did not move an eyelid, but her heart was bursting with pride and joy that her father, so recently converted to Christ, would give such a fearless testimony before this large audience.

Ming had difficulty recovering from the impact of this last statement.

"And isn't it true that your wife and family, and your daughter who attends the university, supported by the taxes of our government, are all Christians?"

Mr. Woo straightened his shoulders and replied politely, "Sir, I am on trial for my faith in Jesus Christ, and I cannot answer for other members of my family or society."

"Dunce! Fool!" he shouted. "Your honor, I rest my case. The defendant has admitted all of the crimes he has been accused of, and I request the court to mete out the proper punishment that will require the re-education of this dunce who is a blight on our society."

With that, the colonel huddled with three other officials seated on the side of the platform. Five minutes passed in almost deathly silence as the audience sat motionless, awaiting the verdict. Finally, the huddle broke and one man stepped forward to read the verdict.

"Guilty on all counts," he said simply, and took his seat.

"Will the defendant stand and face the audience," the colonel said as he looked at his notes. "The court has found the defendant, Woo Mingtao, guilty on all counts. In order to hasten his re-education, he will be sent to serve for a period of ten years in the coal mines of Datong, Shanxi Province."

Mrs. Woo caught her breath, stuffed her handkerchief into her mouth to prevent any outcry. Meiling stiffened with indignation at the injustice done to her father. Tears flooded her eyes, but she did not dare wipe them away.

The colonel stood, and addressing the audience, he said, "Comrades, you have witnessed the trial of this man who has perpetrated his poison on the helpless workers of our new society. His punishment is justified since we must eradicate from society these old-fashioned ideas that he has spread through the years as principal of our high school. I will now call for your agreement with the ruling of the court. All who are in agreement with the ruling that Woo Mingtao should undergo re-education, please raise your right hand."

Once again the crowd was taken by surprise. They were faced with the ugly decision of voting against their friend in order to save their own necks. Prodded by the colonel, people half-heartedly raised their hands, but only a little. Ming and the colonel watched Meiling carefully as she sat stoic and motionless.

"The court takes note, and encourages everyone to remember those who opposed this ruling," added the colonel with a ruthless tone in his voice. "I am sure such individuals will be reminded of their decision at some future date," he threatened as he looked in Meiling's direction. "Now the court is dismissed, and the defendant is immediately remanded to the custody of the police."

Immediately, two policemen jumped to their feet, placed handcuffs on Mr. Woo and led him away as Mrs. Woo watched helplessly. The crowd moved away from Meiling as quickly as possible, making it easy for her to reach her mother who was weeping profusely.

Ming paused as he prepared to leave the hall, and looking at Meiling, he said, "The court took note that you did not agree with the ruling of the People's Court. Be prepared to answer for that some day." Without another word, he turned on his heels and left the building.

Mrs. Woo clung to her daughter and sobbed, "Oh, my poor husband. He did nothing wrong. What will become of him?"

Meiling attempted to comfort her as they walked slowly out of the nearly deserted hall. "Mother, it was horrible what they did, but the angels in heaven are singing praise to the Lord for his testimony. The Lord will be with him," she answered simply.

Two days later as Meiling entered her classroom at the university, she was met by a secretary who handed her a note. Opening it, she read with disbelief that she was expelled from the university because her father was a convicted felon. Having been warned in advance, her classmates and friends had evaporated.

Oh God, she cried from a broken heart, *the cost of following You is staggering. My father has been sent to prison on trumped up charges, and now I am deprived of an education! And, yet, we haven't done anything worthy of this punishment!*

My child, the Lord spoke soothingly, *these present evils are nothing compared to the glory being stored up for those who love Me more than these earthly treasures. And, always remember, My grace is sufficient for all things.*

Wiping the tears from her eyes, she looked up, and there in the doorway was another believer from church. The girl stood motionless with folded arms. Looking Meiling directly in the eye, she cautiously waved her fingers and moved on. Joy flooded Meiling's heart. She was not alone after all. Another believer dared to give her a signal of hope and encouragement.

Hurrying home, she discovered that her brothers and sisters had been likewise expelled from their schools. The Communists were meticulous in these tactics, knowing that the certainty of resisting the new masters brought serious consequences. The public was quickly forced into conformity with their edicts. Their father's conviction had opened up a whole new chapter for the Woo family.

Chapter 11

SAFE IN GOD'S HANDS

rriving at the prison camp entrance, Woo presented his papers to the guard at the gate. "Proceed to that large building over there," he said pointing to an ugly unpainted building about 500 feet away. "The officer in charge will give you directions to your quarters. Good luck, and learn fast. It might help," he added.

Woo picked up his suitcase and bedding roll and walked toward the building. Entering the dismal room, he met the officer sitting behind a scarred desk that had seen better days. Taking his papers, he said listlessly, "Put your bags up on the table so I can check for contraband articles."

Woo opened his suitcase and stood there quietly waiting for the inspection. *What do they consider contraband,* he thought. He didn't have long to wait. Dumping his possessions unceremoniously out on the table, the officer picked up each item, looked it over and tossed it in a heap.

"Paper and pens," he said as he picked up a writing pad. "Not allowed. This is a work camp, not a luxury hotel. Better learn that fast," he said as he continued examining each item. "Ah, and what is this?" he asked as he held up a Bible. "This is definitely contraband and is not allowed," he said with impatience. "One of the reasons you are here is because you are full of old ideas. This is considered a most dangerous book, and it is forbidden."

Opening the Bible, he took a firm grip on each half, tore it apart, and threw it to the floor. "That's what we think about this book," he said defiantly as he trampled on God's Word. "Absolutely forbidden!"

Woo stiffened as his Bible was torn apart and trampled on, but he said nothing. "You won't be using this scarf," the man said as he laid it aside. "You will be issued prison clothes and everything else will be confiscated. There's no room for such things here," he added.

His gloves were thrown on the pile of confiscated articles along with the pictures of his family as the guard simply said, "Not allowed." Half of the contents of his suitcase now lay on the contraband side. "All right, that's it," he said indicating the items he would be allowed to take in. "Wrap them up in something and leave the suitcase here. Not allowed," he added.

Sadly, Woo bundled up his few remaining possessions, and looking longingly for the last time at the precious things taken from him, he followed a young guard to his barracks. *At least they will never be able to take Jesus away from me*, he thought as he followed silently. *My Bible is gone, but I have Christ in my heart. I'm glad now that I took Pastor Yang's advice and started memorizing some passages of Scripture.*

"You've been assigned to bunk number R-32," the young man said as he searched the long row of bunks.

"Here you are," called out the guard as he pointed to a lower bunk. "You're lucky to get a lower one," he said matter-of-factly, and moved on back to the office.

Woo sat down on his bunk and looked around. There was nothing but bare boards; no mattress or cupboard for his possessions. He was alone in the building that housed about 100 men. *I wonder when they get off work,* he thought. *It must be about 4 o'clock now judging from the location of the sun.* It was another three hours before he heard the sound of shuffling feet. The door opened and in trooped a motley, dirty crowd of men in ragged clothing. Their faces told the story of their miserable existence. Thin, bedraggled, silent, and sullen, they moved to their bunks and lay down. No one paid any attention to him as each man, exhausted from twelve long hours in the mines and the long walk from the mine entrance, took advantage of a few minutes of rest.

A man in his forties, but appearing to be closer to sixty, set his foot on Woo's bunk and started to climb up to the top bunk. He paused, looked at Woo from sunken eyes, and asked wearily, "Are you new? When did you get here?"

"My name's Woo," he said, relieved that someone had spoken to him. "I arrived this afternoon."

"Can't say I'm glad you're here because this is hell," he said bitterly. "My name's Fan. We get something they call a meal after awhile when the bell rings," he offered half-heartedly as he climbed up and lay down on the creaking boards. "Have you found the latrine?" he asked. "It's outside at the south end of the building. Just follow your nose."

"It won't be hard to find," the man across the aisle commented, "but don't plan on staying in there very long. You'll suffocate."

Encouraged that at least someone had spoken to him, Woo ventured a question. "Anyone know a Pastor Wong who is supposed to be in this camp?" he asked. "I'd like to meet him."

"Pastor Wong!" several voices exploded. "Do you know him?"

Suddenly the men around him were wide awake. They pumped him with questions. *How do you know him? Where did you meet him? Are you from his native area?* On and on the questions flew at him, hardly giving him a moment to answer.

"Friends," he said as he waved for silence. "Pastor Wong must be very popular around here, but I have never met him.

I've only heard that he might be here. I want to meet him as soon as possible."

"Pastor Wong doesn't sleep in this barracks, but you will meet him in a little while when we go for our meal. He's a very unusual man," said the prisoner above Woo.

Everyone lapsed into silence as their exhaustion took over weary bodies. Sometime later, a bell sounded and the men shifted hurriedly to get up and into line. Woo followed Fan, the man from the top bunk, not knowing what to expect. The weary men shuffled into a stark and barren room with long bare tables and benches. There was nothing to relieve the starkness of the bare room: tables were unpainted, benches were long and wobbly from countless years of use, and the walls were streaked gray with dust and grime. Guards with rifles stood at intervals, shoving prisoners forward to hasten the serving. Filing past the serving area in silence, men grabbed their bowl of rice with a few stringy-looking vegetables on top, and hastily took their places at the table. Gulping down their food like starving animals, the hungry men waited in tense silence for the signal for their table to go back for a second bowl of rice. Most of the time, the food was exhausted before all had received a second helping, but only despairing stares revealed the hurt and pain of these starving men. Woo watched, but was not ready when his table was selected arbitrarily for a second helping. Following the lead of the other men at his table, he got into line with his half full bowl of rice that he continued to eat slowly as was his custom.

Noticing him eating his food as he moved forward with the rest of the men, a young guard stepped up and slapped him in the face, sending his bowl bouncing across the floor.

"Are you the new prisoner here?" he bellowed. "Learn quickly. You don't get in line with food in your bowl. If you have not finished when the signal is given, stay seated. Now get back to your place immediately!"

Woo stumbled back to his table, embarrassed and confused. A sudden wave of loneliness swept over him as he remembered the warmth and comfort of his home. The bleakness of his situation hit him like stormy ocean waves. *Ten years to live with starving animals like this,* he thought, *and this is only the first night! How will I stand it?*

The men returned to their table and took their places in silence as they ate their second bowl more leisurely. Without a word, Fan, the man from the bunk above him, put his half empty bowl down, and silently shoved it over to Woo. He passed him his chopsticks and motioned for him to eat. Taken by surprise, Woo pushed the bowl back toward the emaciated man. *How could I eat this man's food? After all, he had worked all day and must be famished,* he thought. The man gently pushed it back and whispered, "Do as I say or we'll both get into trouble for talking like this."

Grateful, but reluctantly, Woo picked up Fan's chopsticks as he in turn whispered a quiet "Thank you." Fifteen minutes after entering the mess hall, the men filed out for thirty minutes of freedom in the yard surrounding the barracks.

Fan said as they stepped out into the cool air of the night, "You were fortunate the guard only slapped you. Most of the time they use their rifle butts to beat us. In the future, eat as quickly as possible, and be ready if seconds are offered. Not everyone gets a second helping, so you must not miss the opportunity."

"Thank you so much for your kindness in sharing the little food you had. You must be very hungry, and yet you shared it with me. Why did you do that for a stranger?" he asked.

"Because I have been given so much by my Father in heaven," he replied. "It is what Jesus would have done, too."

"Then, you are a believer," Woo replied softly and with great delight. "Is that right?"

"Yes, and you are also a believer. I know you are because I saw you bow your head and give thanks while everyone else gulped down his food. You must ask the blessing immediately in the few minutes before you receive your food," he said with a knowing smile. "That way, you will be ready to eat quickly and perhaps get a second bowl."

"Thank you for your kindness to me. I will learn quickly," he promised. "If you are a believer, then you must know Pastor Wong," he added hopefully.

"Indeed I do," the man replied. "I owe that man my life because he showed me the way to peace in this awful place. You'll meet him soon, I am sure. He's always looking out for newcomers."

The next morning before the sun rose, a long line of prisoners made their way slowly toward the mineshaft.

"Stay seated and keep your head down," warned Fan. "The roof is very low in some places. I have known several men who died on this train because they were not careful. The government does not provide us with helmets either, so watch out for the jagged places in the roof or walls."

The only light was the headlight of the small engine that pulled this train into the bowels of the earth. Many of the men had learned to hunker down in the car and use these minutes of descent into the mine for an extra few minutes of sleep. It paid to conserve as much energy as possible because the day would be long and the work exhausting. Reaching the work area after some fifteen minutes of slow travel into the mine, the crew boss ordered them out of the cars and issued each of them a pick ax with which they were expected to dislodge the coal in the vein they were working on, and load it into the cars.

"Where are the shovels?" Woo asked innocently.

"Ha! Listen to him," one man growled. "There are no shovels. You use your hands! Haven't you noticed how black our hands are?"

"And your hands will be bruised and bleeding before the day is over," said Fan. "This is one of the worst things you'll endure these first days, but gradually your hands will become hardened and it won't be too bad."

The darkness seemed to envelop him and press in upon his lonely heart. His first days were the hardest as he learned what was expected of him. The foreman was a tough taskmaster who made certain that the quota of coal was mined. Before the day was half over, the hands that had never held a pick ax before were throbbing with pain from broken blisters. His hands were a mass of raw flesh.

"These are the worst days," offered Fan who had been assigned to break him in to the rigors of coal mining. "At first, your hands will feel like they are coming off your arms," he said sympathetically. "The only hope I can offer you is to assure you that in a few weeks they will have become calloused and hard like mine, and they won't hurt as much as yours do right now. Tomorrow will be worse than this first day," he added, again with sympathy. "The biggest problem is there is so little water to cleanse your hands, and nothing to soothe the pain. You will just have to bear it. Just watch out for the foreman, though. He is cruel and will show you no mercy. It's part of the education of this school, he always says. And, besides, tonight we must sit for an hour or more of indoctrination and struggle. Learn to say the right words as soon as possible as that will make it easier for you."

"Thank you for your kindness," Woo said as he stretched his aching back and held up his painful hands. "I don't know how I will last until quitting time."

"Whatever you do," said his new friend, "don't show any signs of weakness or that man will heap more work and torture on you. Be careful. Here he comes now," he cautioned quietly as he resumed his work.

"So, you're the new student in my school," the foreman said as he stopped by Woo. "Looks to me like you've never been in a coalmine before. It's the best place to learn the lessons about our New China and purge your mind of the old traditions. But you better be a quick learner or you will not survive here.

He chuckled at his cruel remarks and moved on.

"Not the best welcome for a newcomer," said Fan. "The problem is, he can back up his threats with actions if you cross him. But usually, if we make our quota, he's not too bad."

"I'll do my best."

They worked on in silence and only spoke in whispers when the guards were at a safe distance.

"This is a miserable place to spend your life," Fan offered sometime later, "but ever since I became a believer through Pastor Wong, life has been more bearable. At least I now have a reason to keep on living and I have a hope that goes beyond this life."

"You have mentioned him several times already. He must be a remarkable man."

"He certainly is, but you must be careful because he is a marked man."

"And why is that?"

"Simply because he is so bold in sharing his faith, but once you know him, you can't stay away from him, no matter what the cost may be."

The two men worked side by side all afternoon, speaking only occasionally when they were alone.

"I don't think I can hold out much longer," Woo admitted. "How do you know what time it is down here, and how do you know when the day is over?"

"Good questions," answered his new friend. "About two hours before quitting time, the foreman blows a whistle, and then he comes around and checks each cart to see if it will be filled by quitting time. If he thinks we have been working too slowly, he will use the whip he always carries with him. I've seen a couple of men die under his whip. He's a cruel man."

"And will we be held to the same quota as the other men?" Woo asked realizing that his new friend could be in jeopardy because of him.

"If he thinks the new worker has been working diligently during his first days on the job, he might make an allowance for a smaller quota. By the second week, he is merciless, but don't worry about us. I think we will come out pretty good. You have been doing very well for your first day. You're my buddy for this first week so I think we can get through without difficulty. I'm trying to work a little faster to make up the quota."

"I thought so," Woo replied gratefully. "I noticed you rarely take a rest.

"You would do it for me also, my brother. Some day you will have opportunity to help another newcomer in the mine. It is only by helping each other that we can survive down here. Pastor Wong taught us that."

Conversation stopped as the whistle blew. The men worked harder knowing that the foreman would soon be stopping by their cart. They didn't have long to wait.

"Well, Woo," he said as he looked into the cart. "Either you are a very good worker or your friend here is doing double duty. Looks like you'll almost make the quota for today."

"I'm doing my best," he replied simply.

"Your hands are a mess," said the foreman as he noticed the grimy blood on the pick ax. "I'm going to give you a break today. Both of you, take a rest. You've done an excellent job today." He paused as he started to move on. "But don't think I'm a softy. In three days I expect a full quota or else," he said menacingly.

As he moved on, Fan whispered, "That's a miracle! I never heard him say such a thing before. Brother, the Lord is here in this cold, dark place, and He just proved how much He cares for us. Praise be to His holy name."

That evening during the break time, Fan said, "Come with me. I think I know where to find Pastor Wong."

"There he is," he said as he pointed to a stooped man who looked to be in his mid eighties. "That's Pastor Wong talking with those men over there. Let's join them."

As they approached, Pastor Wong looked up, and with kindly eyes and a strong, steady voice he welcomed Woo.

"Ah, my brother, you were given a harsh welcome to this place last evening, but do not fear, Jesus is here," he said reassuringly. The other men smiled in agreement. One spoke up and added, "And God has this angel here to help us through these bitter days of our lives so that we can endure."

"Pastor Wong, my name is Woo. I have been waiting to meet you."

"I take it you are a believer also," he responded enthusiastically. "We cannot speak openly here about Jesus and our faith, but we manage to find one another and share a few thoughts we have gleaned from God's Word."

"Oh, then you have Bibles?" Woo asked in surprise. "The guard confiscated my Bible and tore it apart when I arrived."

"I am sorry to hear that, but no Bibles are allowed in, and every one of them has been confiscated. The only Bible we have is what is in our hearts—the chapters we have memorized. While you were free, did you memorize any Scripture?" he enquired.

"I am a new believer of only a few months," Woo replied, "but I took my pastor's advice and started memorizing Scripture."

"Excellent. It is the only thing that sustains us in this awful place. Whenever we have a few minutes with one another, we quote Scripture and store it up in our hearts. We have been reviewing 2 Corinthians 2:14 'But thanks be to God, who always leads us in triumphal procession in Christ and through us spreads the knowledge of him.'"

"That's a new one. I will work on it," Woo replied gratefully.

As Pastor Wong quietly encouraged the small group of men huddled around him, a whistle blew announcing the end of the free period.

"I'll probably see you down below," encouraged Pastor Wong as the men quickly separated and returned to their barracks. "Remember, Jesus is here. He never forsakes us."

As Woo crawled into his bunk a few minutes later, there was little conversation as the tired men gave in to their weariness.

It was pitch dark when the morning whistle blew, awakening the men for a new day's work. Woo rolled out like the others, and followed the men to the washing area. Morning needs were easily completed within the ten minutes allotted, and all were in line to march to the mess hall for a thin bowl of gruel.

"Lick the bowl clean," a man advised Woo. "You won't get much else until tonight, so don't waste a drop."

Finishing his breakfast quickly just as the others, he fell into line for the long march to the mine entrance. It was much colder here in Datung than in Puyang and the prison garb didn't do much to keep out the cold wind. *What will it be like when winter arrives,* he thought with a shudder. *Why did they need to take my scarf?* His thoughts were interrupted as Pastor Wong fell in step with him.

"Good morning, Brother Woo. And, how did you sleep last night?"

"Apart from missing my family, I slept quite well," he answered, "considering the strange surroundings."

"I prayed for you last night. The first days are always the hardest because of all the unknown things that are happening around you. But you will get used to it, and with the help of the Lord, you will survive. I have been here for three years already, but I still have seventeen to go. I am resigned to the fact that I will go from here to see my Jesus whom I love very much."

"May I ask how old you are, brother?" asked Woo.

"By the grace of God, I am seventy-nine years old and praising Him for every breath that He allows me, although I must confess that life in this camp has been taking its toll on my body. Working in the mines these three years with the dampness and low ceilings, has caused my rheumatism to be a constant source of pain. But Brother Woo, it is out of my pain that God gives me the opportunities to share my faith with the men here who do not know Him."

"How is it that you are permitted to share your faith like this? I thought it was forbidden to spread the gospel."

"It is against the rules, but there are lots of openings God gives me to share the good news. I just wait for an opportunity."

The two men talked quietly as they walked along the dark road. In the days that followed, the two became daily companions in the walk to the mine entrance. At night, there was less talk, as they were weary from the hard labor of the day.

"I have been an itinerant preacher for twenty years," Pastor Wong revealed one morning, "and my travels have taken me up and down throughout this land. Much of my time has been spent up north in areas dominated by the Communists, and it was a constant struggle to stay out of their way."

"They must have caught you in a secret meeting somewhere. Is that right?"

"Yes," he replied sadly. "I was traveling in an area where the people were very hungry for God's Word. Each night, we met in a different home. The believers gathered late at night to avoid the police, but one night I was betrayed by a man who pretended to desire to know the way. He betrayed me in order to save his own neck. We had just started our meeting, when the secret police arrived and beat me in front of the congregation. They tore up our Bibles and hymn books, and arrested quite a few of us that night.

Only the elder of the church and I were detained for several weeks. I believe he was given a prison term also. But that is what Jesus said would happen. 'You will be arrested,' He said, 'and turned over to the authorities for my sake, and they will beat you and put you in prison for my sake, but don't worry about what you will say at such times.' Remember, Jesus said, 'I will put my words in your mouth and give you wisdom to know what to do.' Oh, Brother Woo, it is all true! Jesus is here in this camp, and He helps me each day to continue spreading the good news."

"Do you ever get discouraged and lonely in this place?" he asked.

"I would not be honest if I said I am never lonely or discouraged; but when I am, Jesus comes and walks beside me, and He comforts me."

"No wonder the men love you so much," exclaimed Woo. "I hope I can be like you and help men here in this prison."

"Just let God have full sway in your life, my dear brother," responded the pastor. They were so engrossed in their conversation, they did not notice a guard moving along the line, prodding the men to walk faster.

"Stop talking," he shouted at the two of them as he took the end of his rifle and poked Woo vigorously in the ribs. He caught his breath as the pain surged through his body. Except for the steadying hand of Pastor Wong, he would have stumbled and fallen. They continued on in silence to the entrance of the mine. There, they boarded empty coal cars and started into the darkness. When they got to the end of the line where they were to begin working, Woo suddenly noticed the old pastor's hands.

"Forgive me for asking this question," Woo said hesitantly, "but I just noticed that you only have stubs for fingers. Did you suffer an accident here in the mines?"

"The coal is very sharp at times. These things happen, he replied softly. "But Brother Woo, every time I look at my hands, I think of the hands of Jesus that were wounded for me on the cross. It helps me bear the pain because He bore so much more for me."

What a remarkable man he is, thought Woo as he still struggled to get the hang of chipping away at the coal vein. When a pile had accumulated, he gathered up a handful and dumped it in the empty car. Filling a car by nightfall was a burdensome task, but if it wasn't accomplished, the whole crew working on that car suffered.

At noon, they were given some time to rest, and a hard stale portion of Chinese steam bread. The men ate more slowly than at the table, and lingered over each bite, savoring the taste as long as possible. A large container of tea was also provided; the only drink available throughout the entire day. Tea never tasted any better in his comfortable home than this cupful out of a tin cup that probably hadn't ever been washed.

"They treat us like animals," Pastor Wong commented, "but I remember who I am in Christ. I'm the child of the King." With a joyous lilt in his voice he said, "And no guard or government can deny me my privileges in Him."

"You are a remarkable man, Pastor Wong," exclaimed Woo as the warning whistle announced that the rest period was almost over.

"No, I am not remarkable, Brother Woo. My Jesus is remarkable and extraordinary, and He sustains me hour by hour."

"You," the guard in the mine spoke up roughly, "quit the talk and get back to work."

"Ah, praise the Lord," Pastor Wong said as the guards disappeared from the area. "Now, we can have some time to worship the Lord together. Just keep working, though, so we make our quota. Let's just praise the Lord for His mercy and goodness to us."

"How do you manage to be so joyful day after day in this awful place?" Woo asked. "Yesterday, I cut my hand badly, but I was refused any medical help. Look at it. It's swollen and very painful. I don't feel like praising the Lord," he confessed honestly.

"Ah, my brother," Pastor Wong replied sympathetically, "joy is not the result of good circumstances, but because Jesus is dwelling in us. It is His joy that fills us every day and gives us peace no matter where we are. Of course, we suffer pain in this place, but we also lean hard on Jesus. He carries the load, and we walk beside Him held in His mighty hand. Let's pray together as we work."

With that he launched into a fervent prayer as he continued scooping up the coal he had broken loose from the vein they were working on. His cries to God were no less fervent because his eyes were open and his hands were busy loading the coal. He implored God to sooth Woo's hand and heal the wound in spite of the lack of treatment.

When he finished praying, Woo spoke softly. "You have helped to make this place bearable and given me so much hope in spite of my circumstances."

"And may I add," said Pastor Wong, "that I have been encouraged by you. Your desire to be all that God wants of you in this place encourages me to go on reaching out to others here even though it could cause me some discomfort and probably prolong my time in this mine. But what does it matter; I am already an old man. I don't have much time left on this earth, so I will use it all to serve my Lord."

Chapter 12

THE IRON-CLAD HEEL

Flushed with victory over Mr. Woo, Colonel Ching, the ruthless political leader of Hubei Province, proceeded almost immediately to bring the churches under his control. The Religious Affairs Bureau had been functioning for many months by this time, but the pressure to conform had been gradual. Churches were restricted from conducting Sunday schools, and pastors had to submit their sermons for approval. Now the iron-clad heel of the government crunched down with a vengeance unheard of in the past. Pastors and elders were faced with a growing number of edicts, all designed to eventually wipe out every vestige of Christianity and other religions from the country. Day by day, the evil design became more obvious: squeeze the church and leaders until there was no life left in them.

The edict demanding all churches to register with the Religious Affairs Bureau under a plan, called the Three-Self Patriotic Movement, would eventually be the one that would close all church doors. It purported to bring freedom from the management of foreign denominations, freedom from the slavery and control of foreign money, and freedom to propagate the church according to Chinese style and control. Unfortunately, the real plan was to close all churches throughout the entire country and bring about the re-edu-cation of pastors and leaders to conform to Communist ideology.

Pastor Yang had made a fair recovery from his brutal beatings at the hands of the police, but he confided to his wife that he knew that every day the noose was tightening around his neck.

"My dear wife," he said one day with a deep sigh as they sat together in their living room, "everyone knows the stand I have taken pits me against the government, but I want you to know that no matter what happens, I will never willingly renounce Jesus, my Lord. I cannot submit to the godless reforms the Religious Affairs Bureau is pushing. You must be prepared to go on without me. I am sure my days are numbered and the severest test of my life is about to begin."

"Oh, Chiwah," she responded with tears in her eyes. "I told you at that first meeting in Hankou that I would rather be a widow than be married to a coward who renounced his faith to save his life. Yes, it will be very difficult, but our God reigns and He is victor. I will trust Him no matter what happens, and He will see us through. Only do not renounce your faith in Jesus for my sake. So many people are watching you. You are their model, their guide, through these troubled waters."

"You are a brave woman and a great support to me," he answered honestly as he gripped her hand. "You are right. Jesus will see us through whatever lies ahead, and He will bring us out of this fiery trial as pure gold."

A few weeks after this conversation, as they were sitting quietly reading the Bible together, they heard a great commotion at the front gate of the church. The sound of angry voices demanding entrance filled the night air. Pastor Yang had just completed reading Psalm 46 and was remarking to his wife that the Lord would be their refuge in times of trouble. Startled by the noise, he paused, looked at the clock, and noted that it was 9:35 P.M. Nighttime was when the police frequently chose to make an arrest. The gatekeeper's wife rushed in as her husband slowly prepared to open the gate. The pounding on the gate was deafening, and the angry shouts sent chills up their spines.

"The police are at the gate," she whispered in fear. "They will be here in a minute. Hide, pastor, hide," she cried.

"No, I have been expecting them these many weeks. Do not be afraid of what they can do to our bodies, but always remember, they cannot touch our souls!"

As the gate slowly opened, the police pushed the old gatekeeper aside, and rushed to the Yang's apartment.

"Are you Pastor Yang?" the police officer questioned rudely. "You are ordered to come with me to the police station."

"I am ready," he replied quietly. "I have been expecting you for many weeks. My bag is all packed and ready," he said as he reached behind a chair and picked up a small suitcase. Picking up his Bible, he proceeded to put it into the bag.

"Is that a Bible?" the policeman asked angrily as he grabbed it from the pastor's hand. "You are not permitted to take this with you," he said as he read the characters *Holy Bible* on the cover. "It is against the law to read this book of the counter-revolutionaries. If you know what is good for you, you will concentrate on Chairman Mao's Red Book of quotations. That is all you need!"

Then with a vicious gleam in his eyes, he ripped the Bible in two, threw it to the floor and repeatedly stamped on it as the Yangs watched in horrified silence. He ground his heel into the book until the pages were in tatters. Then with a wicked grin he said, "There! That's what we think of your holy book. It is worthless and will be destroyed. Our people will no longer be duped by this foreign trash of the imperialists." And, then, as if to heap more insult on the Yang's, he spit on the Bible and kicked it across the room.

"Handcuff him," he ordered, "and take him away."

As Pastor Yang moved slowly toward the door, he paused, looked deep into his wife's eyes, and whispered, "The Lord is with us and He will take care of us. Just pray for me to be strong."

"Move ahead," the policeman shouted as he gave him a rough push.

Pushed into the bare, stark room where the chief of police sat at a desk, Pastor Yang was reminded of the last time he stood there.

"So we meet again," began the chief with an evil grin on his face. "I thought by this time, Yang, that you would have learned your lesson and accepted our great leader's policies to make China a great nation free from the superstition of religion! And by the way, you don't need to tell me the names of your elders. I know who they are and where they live. You see, not all of the people who attend your church are as foolish as you are. They value their freedom and they provide me with regular information on your activities. And, judging from this file, you have not been observing the new regulations!"

He put the thick file on the desk in front of him and thumbed through the pages.

"I see here from my informant that you have been teaching the people that this Jesus will some day come back to earth and become the king of all the nations. Is it true that you have been teaching such unfounded ideas to the people?"

Pastor Yang stood erect as he responded quietly, "I have told you before that I am a loyal Chinese citizen, and I do not teach any subversive teachings to the people. What this report refers to is the teaching of the Bible that Jesus Christ, who is the true and living God, will some day return to earth and rule as the righteous king of all the nations. In that day, there will be world-wide peace and happiness everywhere."

"Then you admit that this report is accurate?" he said as he jumped to his feet, walked over to Pastor Yang, and slapped him in the face. "Didn't I warn you the last time you were here that you must give up these silly notions about Jesus and begin to follow the instructions of our great leader, Chairman Mao? When will you begin to understand that this is the New China and we have new ideas for the world?"

"The teaching that Jesus Christ will some day rule the world as King of kings and Lord of lords does not make me a poor Chinese citizen, but a better one," declared Pastor Yang. "Jesus taught us how to love one another, and even to love our enemies and to help them. You will discover that Christians are good citizens and they will help our nation become great and strong."

"Nonsense!" he shouted. "Where is this Jesus? Have you ever seen him?"

"Jesus is in heaven," Pastor Yang answered as he licked the blood from his lip. "Although I have not seen Him with my eyes, I know He is alive and He lives in my life."

The conversation continued for an hour, punctuated every once in a while with a vicious slap to the face. Pastor Yang's eyes were swollen and his face puffed, but he stood firmly on God's Word, giving faithful testimony.

"You are hopeless, Yang," screamed the chief. "I will see you in the morning and give you another chance to renounce this stupid religion. In the meantime, stand where you are until I return."

Turning to the guards standing nearby, he ordered, "Make certain that he remains standing until I return," and with that he stamped out of the room.

The minutes slowly turned into hours as Pastor Yang fought exhaustion. Shifting from one foot to the other, he tried to relieve the pressure on his aching back. Finally, sleep overcame him, and he crumpled to the floor. Immediately, the guards rushed to him, and while they fiercely kicked him awake, they pulled him to his feet, and demanded that he stand. The torture was almost unbearable as his body cried out for relief. As he stood there he was reminded of Jesus in Pilate's judgment hall, battered and beaten by the savage soldiers. In that moment, he seemed to feel an arm lift him up and support him. Relief swept through his body. *Thank You, Jesus,* he prayed silently, *I know You are here to sustain me. Help me to be strong for You and honor Your name through my life.*

The hours passed quickly after that, and when the guards changed at 6 A.M., they looked at Pastor Yang with amazement as one said to the other, "What kind of a man is this who can stand all night and look so peaceful?"

At eight o'clock, the chief entered the room and found Pastor Yang still standing where he left him the night before.

"Yang," he said, "I have told you before that I am not a bad man. I am only carrying out my orders. You will make it easier for me if you do as I ask," he said almost pleadingly. "And to show you that I am not as bad as you think, I will allow you to be seated. Guard, bring a chair for this man," he ordered.

Seated before the chief who was eating his breakfast in front of Pastor Yang as an additional means of torture, the chief further taunted him by reminding him that he too could have a nourishing breakfast if he would only renounce his faith in Jesus.

"Why don't you give up this nonsensical faith in a foreign religion and join me in persuading the people to follow our great leader, Chairman Mao?" he asked over and over again. "You could live in luxury by simply joining the Party and helping me," he offered.

"Sir," responded Pastor Yang again and again, "I could never give up my faith in Jesus Christ. He means everything to me. As long as I have any strength left in me, I will never desert my Lord."

"You are a fool, Yang," shouted the chief as he slammed his cup down on the desk for emphasis. "Why would you endure such suffering for this Jesus that no one can prove even exists?"

"Sir," replied Pastor Yang politely, and yet with assurance in his voice, "I know, and thousands of Chinese believers know beyond a shadow of a doubt that Jesus is alive in heaven, and that He is the true and living God. He lives within us and helps us through every trial and difficulty. Believe me, we will all die for Jesus, and I assure you that you will never be able to overcome the church."

The chief looked at him in amazement. For a few moments he sat there speechless, and then his anger began to boil over.

"How dare you assume that the People's Republic of China does not have the power to obliterate whatever it chooses! The church thrives on the superstitious beliefs of the people and it has no power against us. They will die, and the church will be wiped out," he said with finality. "Now, I will give you one more chance to renounce your faith, or I have the means to force you to do so," he said as his eyes flashed with a steely glint. "What is your decision?"

"Sir, I will never give up my Jesus. He means everything to me!"

"Guard," bellowed the chief, "get this fool out of my presence. Send him home immediately!" And turning to Pastor Yang, he continued sternly, "Yang, you are a fool if ever I saw one. Go home and get ready for the test of your life. I doubt if you will pass this one!"

Stunned and bewildered by the strange turn of events, Pastor Yang returned home to his wife, and relayed to her the order.

"What do you think he meant?" she asked anxiously.

"I have no idea, but I believe we will find out very soon. Now is the time as never before, that I need the prayers of Christ's body so that I can pass the test, whatever it will be."

Sunday morning dawned bright and clear as many people began gathering early for the service. They made their way to one
of the prayer groups and prayed for a mighty demonstration of
God's power.

"Give us boldness, O God," they prayed, "to proclaim Your
Word. Demonstrate Your mighty power on behalf of Your people.
Let Your name be magnified through our lives no matter what
the cost."

No one realized how soon their prayers would be answered.

Every pew in the church was filled to capacity as people tried to
squeeze an extra body in where there was no longer any room.
Latecomers were disappointed as they crowded the lobby area,
straining their necks to catch a view of the service underway.
Unexpectedly, a commotion broke out in the lobby. Screaming
people were pushed aside by the heavily armed police who rushed
in and headed for the platform. Cries of dismay arose in the congregation as memories of Pastor Yang being arrested a few weeks
earlier flooded their minds. Those nearest the door fled from the
expected conflict, only to be stopped by the police who had surrounded the building.

Pastor Yang looked down from the platform to see the chief of
police boldly walking down the aisle toward him.

"Yang," he shouted rudely as he proceeded toward the platform, "get ready for the test of your life! I told you to be ready.
Come with me to the river and bring your whole congregation
with you. Now we'll see if your Jesus will help you."

Two policemen flanked Pastor Yang and marched him out of
the church.

"The rest of you," shouted the chief, "follow Yang to the river, and don't try to run away or you'll be shot."

The muddy waters of the mighty Yangtze River flowed just one mile from the church. Pastor Yang was hastened along with several hundred people following, their hearts filled with apprehension and fear. *What does all this mean? What are they going to do to our pastor?* Many prayed silently for God to be magnified no matter what happened. Reaching the river, the police ushered him out on a pier where a chair was standing with a heavy rope attached. Motioning Pastor Yang to sit in the chair, the chief proceeded to interrogate him.

"Yang," he said pompously, "you have been a thorn in my side for many months. I have been very patient with you, but you have resisted all of the opportunities for re-education. Now today, I will give you one more chance to renounce this Jesus you call your God, and before all of these people, tell them to give up following this foreign, imperialistic religion. If you do not renounce this foolishness, and urge your people to follow our great leader, Chairman Mao, then you will be immersed in this river. You will have a few seconds to change your mind while under the water, and when we bring you back up, you can go free if you renounce your faith. Now, are you ready to give up this foolish religion or must I persuade you before all your people?"

"Sir," Pastor Yang replied in a clear voice for his whole congregation to hear, "I love Jesus with all my heart. I will never renounce Him. He means everything to me."

Enraged, the chief ordered him to be tied into the chair that was then hoisted out over the river.

"Yang," he shouted, "will you renounce Jesus and follow Chairman Mao?"

"Jesus means everything to me. I will never renounce Him," he replied without a moment's hesitation.

"Lower him into the river," ordered the chief.

"No," shouted the people. "Stop. You must not do this," they cried.

Paying no attention to the shouting people, the chair was lowered until the water reached Pastor Yang's neck. Mrs. Yang was forced to stand close by and watch this cruel torture. Her lips moved in silent prayer as other women clung to her.

"Tell him to give up," one whispered. "He will drown if he doesn't!"

"How can you say that?" she asked. "It is better to die for Jesus than save your skin. Eternal life awaits him. They can only kill his body, but never his soul," she responded bravely.

"Yang, you have one more chance," shouted the chief.

"Jesus means more to me than anything else in this world. I will never renounce Him," he called out as the water lapped at his chin.

"Then lower him into the water," ordered the chief.

People gasped as the pastor's head went under the water. Many began to call upon the Lord to preserve their pastor and save him from a watery grave. He prayed also. *Lord, this may be the moment when I lay down my life for you. Help me now to be faithful. Help me to survive for Your glory!"* Fifteen seconds passed, sixteen, seventeen, eighteen! His lungs were crying out for a breath of air. *Can I hold out? Will they pull me up?* he thought. *Jesus, help me,* he prayed as he felt the chair begin to move upward. In another moment, his head broke through the water as he gasped and sucked in some air. *Ah, how good it felt to breathe again!* As the chair swung at the end of the rope, his people looked on in horror. They broke into a loud cry of joy when they saw that he was still alive. The chief gazed at the people and glared at them in anger, but he was not finished yet.

"Yang," he called, "are you ready to renounce this Jesus?"

Sucking in the fresh air, he called down from the chair swinging at the end of the rope, "Sir, I told you, Jesus means everything to me. I will never renounce Him."

"Lower him again," he shouted angrily. "Give him forty-five seconds this time!"

Oh, dear God, help me to be faithful unto death, he prayed. He had never stopped to think how long forty-five seconds under water would be! *Could he hold out?* With lungs crying out for air, he thought, *This is it. Lord, receive me into Your arms.* The congregation stood silent, praying fervently for their pastor. As he burst out of the water again, they could not contain their joy as they saw him gasp, shake his head, and take deep breaths.

"You idiots," shouted the chief at the crowd. "You are here to witness the strength of our great Communist government. No one is willing to give up his life for this Jesus. Watch how we will win!" he shouted. "And if you give this man support any longer, you, too, will be arrested and tested."

The crowd sobered at these threats, but one courageous man shouted out, "You can only kill our bodies, but we will live forever in heaven with Jesus. He is victor."

"Arrest him," shouted the chief. "I will teach him who is strongest: Jesus or the government."

Turning to Pastor Yang, he shouted fiercely with curses and oaths, "Yang, renounce your faith or you will be submerged again!"

"I will never give up my Jesus. He means everything to me," he called down weakly from the swinging chair. "I will give my life for Jesus."

"Lower him into the water," the chief ordered in disgust.

A whisper swept through the crowd. *Oh, not again! He won't survive another time!* People looked at their watches. The second hands moved so slowly. *Oh, God,* they prayed, *help our pastor now.* They counted slowly in soft whispers, *40, . . . 41 . . . 42 . . . 45 . . . Can he hold out?* they thought.

"Pull him up! Pull him up," cried out an old woman. "He'll drown," she called out as she wept.

The crowd counted as they prayed, *46 . . . 47 . . . 48 . . .*

Down under the water, Pastor Yang's temples throbbed. His lungs screamed for air. *I can't hold out. Lord, I'm coming home!*

The chief watched his watch. *Forty-eight seconds. Can he hold out this long?* he thought. *Better bring him up. I don't want him dying here in public,* raced through his mind.

"Bring him up," he ordered, fearful of what he might have done. *My superiors might not look with favor on doing this in public,* he reasoned as he urged his men to pull harder. Pastor Yang felt the upward surge. *If I can only hold out a few seconds more,* he prayed. *Hurry! Hurry! I can't hold much longer!* His head broke through the water as he gulped in a deep breath. His head fell to his chest in exhaustion. The people moaned as they saw their beloved pastor's head fall on his chest.

The men worked fast, pulling the chair over to the pier as the chief ordered them to untie the pastor quickly. Lifting him out of the chair, they laid him on the rough planks of the pier. He lay there a few moments. Then his eyes fluttered open! Word spread rapidly that he was alive. The people dared not express their joy other than quietly saying under their breath, *"Praise the Lord. Oh, praise the Lord!"*

"Yang," a subdued chief said, "get up and go home, and re-member today's lesson. It would be best if you renounced this Jesus you so stubbornly believe in, or something worse will happen to you to help you learn faster."

Chapter 13

IT HAD TO BE GOD

With Mr. Woo sentenced to ten years in the coalmines of Datung, the fortunes of the family changed rapidly. Mrs. Woo was forced to move out of the family home, and Meiling found a job in the local hospital doing the most menial tasks, such as cleaning bedpans and washing dirty laundry, but she also attracted the attention of the hospital administrator.

"Come work for me and give me what I want, and your salary will be increased to 300 yuan a month!"

"I am a Christian," Meiling responded bravely. "I will never be involved in any immoral situation no matter how much money is offered."

Furious with her response, he threatened her with reprisals unless she submitted to his wishes.

"God has placed you in that hospital to be His witness," her mother said one morning as they prayed together. "I have that same assurance in my heart about your father in Datung. Last night, when I could not sleep, thinking about the terrible conditions he must be enduring, the Lord spoke to me and assured me that He was right there with him."

"Really, mother?" Meiling responded eagerly. "What did the Lord say to you?"

"I had gotten out of bed, and was kneeling by my bed weeping, when suddenly I sensed the presence of the Lord there with me. He tenderly touched my shoulder and said, 'Don't weep, my daughter, your dear husband is safe for I have prepared a special place for him, and given him some Christian companions to help him. Remember my Word that says when I put forth my sheep, I go before them and care for them? I am victor over every circumstance.' Oh, Meiling, His presence was so real I just knelt there for more than two hours. The Lord assured me that though we all pass through deep waters, they will not overwhelm us."

"Oh, praise the Lord for this word of encouragement. With Father in the coalmines, and not one word from Anching for so many years, and with that administrator constantly threatening me, Satan has been tempting me to take the easy road! Your words have strengthened me to face today and the coming trouble with the administrator."

"My dear child," Mrs. Woo continued, "we must rely upon God's Word, for it has never failed. Remember, Pastor Yang has urged us to trust in the Lord at all times and not to lean on our own understanding. Now is the time to put that into practice."

Reassured and comforted, Meiling started off to the hospital as dawn was breaking, with a song in her heart and the knowledge that she was under His loving wing. About mid-morning, her supervisor approached her saying, "You have been chosen by Mr. Ma for an advancement because of your excellent work," she began. "You will be moving upstairs to work as his personal assistant."

A slight smile crossed her face. Meiling's heart sank as fear gripped her heart momentarily.

"Your salary will be increased to 300 yuan a month, which is twice as much as I make," she continued without looking directly at Meiling. "You will report at 8 A.M. each day and enjoy some evenings out as well. Do you have any questions?" she asked in such a way as to say, *but don't you dare ask any.*

To the supervisor's surprise, Meiling responded by saying, "Mr. Ma made that offer a few days ago, but I will not be involved with him in any illicit arrangement. My answer a few days ago was 'No,' and it still is!"

"You have no choice," replied the shocked woman. "You will report for your new work in the morning or be severely punished for insubordination," she replied curtly, her sweet tone abruptly changing. "And now, you are excused."

"But . . ." she began.

The supervisor cut her short with an exasperated command. "Get out of here, you idiot. That's more money than I make at this job! With your father in prison for anti-government ideas, you ought to be grateful for any job, or is it your religion that prevents you from doing this work?" she replied sarcastically.

Meiling hesitated a moment, and breathing a prayer she answered boldly. "I am a follower of Jesus Christ. I will never willingly do anything that is immoral or impure just for money."

"No one refuses Mr. Ma's requests," she stated flatly as she tried to control her anger. "You will be in my office here tomorrow at 6 A.M. or suffer the consequences. You Christians had better understand quickly that your objections will always be overruled. We are living in the New China now."

The supervisor stood up, opened the door, and shoved her out. The door slammed shut leaving Meiling standing stunned and shaken in the hall.

"What was that all about?" her friends asked as they gathered around. "You have no choice! You're at his mercy," they all echoed when they heard the story. "For 300 yuan a month, I would do it," said one woman enviously. "In fact, I'd do it for half that amount!"

"I would rather die than yield," Meiling responded firmly. "I am a follower of Jesus. I will never yield to this man's evil lust."

"You're crazy, Meiling. Think what 300 yuan a month means!" "To accept would mean I'd have to deny Jesus as my Lord,"

Meiling replied. "But wait and see what my God will do to deliver me," she replied confidently. Everyone looked at her in amazement. How could this beautiful girl be so confident? "Go to prison?" one questioned. "Yes, if that's necessary."

Exactly at six the next morning, the supervisor's door opened, and the burly woman motioned her inside.

"Well," she began in a very businesslike manner, "I see you've listened to reason. You will report to Mr. Ma's office at 8 A.M. today to begin work. Just do whatever he asks, and you will have no problems at all. Do you understand?"

"Yes, I do," responded Meiling, "but you should know that I will not be involved in any immoral activities with Mr. Ma, regardless of the consequences."

The supervisor sat there stunned for a moment.

"Do you understand what you are saying?" she asked incredulously. "No one questions the authority of the state. You do as you are ordered, or you suffer the consequences."

"I am prepared to do work as a secretary, a servant or an errand girl, but I will not serve him in any other manner."

The supervisor stood up, and with a menacing look on her face, she walked over to her and slapped her so hard it spun her around.

"Listen to me, you idiot. You will do whatever he asks."

She struck Meiling again, opening a cut on her lip. "I will not tolerate your insolence," she screamed. "I have been ordered to prepare you to serve Mr. Ma in any way he pleases, and you will not refuse. I don't care about your Jesus or your religion. You will obey or be punished until you do."

Two quick slaps on each side of her face followed this outburst. Meiling reeled and felt faint.

"I will not submit to his lust and immorality," she spoke firmly, though with difficulty, through her rapidly swelling lips.

"You will, you wretched dog," rasped the supervisor. "And to make sure that you will, you will spend the next three days in solitary confinement in total darkness. You may be released any time you decide to obey my orders," she said as she rang a bell for a guard. "Take her to the psychiatric ward and confine her to cell 35 in total darkness," she ordered.

Looking at Meiling she continued, "Total darkness for three days, and one meal a day! That will help you understand that you don't disobey the orders of Mr. Ma."

As Meiling emerged from the supervisor's office, her co-workers stared at her bloodied face and stood silently as she passed by with the guard.

A few minutes later, she was pushed into cell 35. The door slammed shut. Standing in total darkness, she tried to get her bearings. Then, groping her way forward to a wall, she moved slowly around the room until she discovered a bed and sat down on the hard boards. There was no mattress and no bedding—only bare boards. She rested there a few moments as she licked her swollen lips. Her face stung from the blows, but in her heart there was a song of praise to God that she was counted worthy to suffer.

The darkness in Cell 35 pressed unmercifully in on Meiling as she lay on the hard boards. She stared into the darkness, wondering how she would survive three days of this torture. It wasn't long until Satan's subtle voice whispered in her ears, reminding her how stupid she was to hold such high standards and refuse such high pay. *Surely,* he said, *God will understand that you have been forced to do this! After all, the most important thing is to save your life,* he said subtly.

She spoke out loud in the darkness. "Satan, the Bible says that I am to love my God with all my heart, all my soul and with all my body. I have given Jesus my life and that includes my body. It is to be a living sacrifice for Him."

His whispering ceased immediately. *Praise God, Satan fled at the Word!* She began to sing a song of praise to the Lord who is our refuge in times of trouble. Her heart was lifted even though the darkness was oppressive. Exhausted from the ordeal of the morning and the beating she had taken, she eventually drifted off in a peaceful sleep. She awakened with a start as a light came on in her cell and the door creaked opened. An older woman stood there with a tray in her hands and spoke gently to her.

"It is time for your meal," she said as she set the tray down on the end of the bed.

Meiling sat up, blinked several times as her eyes adjusted to the light. Looking around the dingy room, she noticed that there was nothing in it except the bed boards and a bucket for toilet purposes standing in a corner.

"Oh, thank you," Meiling finally said. "Can you tell me what time it is?"

"It is 3 o'clock," the older woman responded. "Oh, your face is bruised," she added sympathetically. "What happened to you, and why are you here?"

Encouraged by the woman's sympathetic tone of voice, she replied, "I have refused to obey an order to become the mistress of the hospital administrator," she said simply, being careful not to say too much to this unknown woman.

"Ah, he's a wicked man," she replied without hesitation. "You are not the first one he has humiliated. But tell me, why have you refused?"

"I am a Christian," she responded boldly.

"Good for you," replied the old woman. "So am I. Be strong in the Lord," she whispered softly. "He will not forsake you."

"You are a believer?" Meiling asked joyfully.

"Yes, I am, and now I remember who you are. I have seen you at Pastor Yang's church. Aren't you the daughter of Mr. Woo, the principal of our high school?"

"Yes, I am," she replied. "Oh, how comforting to meet you. Jesus sent you to encourage me and help me at this time."

"Oh, thank the Lord," she replied happily. "But you only have thirty minutes to eat your food and take care of your toilet needs. Then I must put out the light again. I dare not disobey," she said regretfully.

"I understand," Meiling replied. "You have brought me more than food; you have brought me hope in the midst of this darkness. I will be all right. Just pray for me, and if you can, send a message to my mother and tell her where I am. She has no idea what has happened to me."

"Tell me where she lives and I will get the message to her tonight."

"Oh, thank you so much. You are an angel sent from heaven to help me."

Thirty minutes later, the woman gave her a final word of encouragement. "I must put the light out again," she said sorrowfully, "but remember, the Lord is here with you."

As the steel door shut, the light went out and she was plunged into total darkness again. Panic seized her heart at first, and she wanted to scream out in terror. Then, the words of the woman flooded her mind, 'You are not alone. The Lord is with you.'

Yes, You're right here with me, dear Jesus. I sense Your presence here. Oh, thank You, I am not alone.

There was nothing to do but lie quietly, quote Scripture, pray and meditate on God. It kept her mind from the fearful thoughts of cockroaches and spiders! She hated them in daylight, but facing the unknown in total darkness was extreme torture except that the sweet presence of Jesus settled her mind and kept her peaceful.

She didn't know how long she lay there meditating about the Lord and heaven. Suddenly, she was overwhelmed with a strong compulsion to pray for Anching. *How strange.* The thought startled her. It had been several years since she had last seen him, and although she always thought of him, she never before had this strong urge to pray for him. *What is happening to him right now,* she thought, *that brought this unexpected urge to pray for him? Is he in some special danger?*

She had no way of knowing, of course, that he was actually in grave danger at this very moment in the refugee camp in Hong Kong. Stabbed several times, he clung by a single thread to the fragile cord of life. It seemed like hours that she wrestled in prayer for whatever problem he was facing. As she prayed, she was more convinced than ever that he was alive somewhere and he needed her prayers. After a long while, the burden eased, and she fell into a peaceful sleep.

When she awakened again, she prayed again for Anching. It lifted her spirit and settled the anxiety in her heart. And so the hours passed—praying, meditating on Scripture and sleeping.

She was aroused as a key was inserted in the steel door and the light came on. There beside her bed was the old woman. She reached inside her blouse and pulled out an orange.

"How are you child?" she asked as she offered her the treat. "You made it through the night all right?" she inquired.

"Oh, thank you. Thank you," Meiling responded as she took the orange. "You told me last night that I was not alone; that Jesus was here with me. You were right, and I had sweet communion with Him. I actually feel rested and better than yesterday," she said as a smile lit up her still swollen face.

"Oh, praise the Lord," whispered the woman. "I delivered the message to your mother and we prayed together. Now I must leave lest I be discovered here, but I'll be back with your meal later today. Be of good cheer, my child. Jesus will not forsake you."

The light went out as the door closed silently behind the woman. Oh, what a comfort the light had been for those few minutes. *It will all be over by tomorrow,* she thought, *and I can make it with You, dear Jesus.*

The third day of Meiling's incarceration in solitary confinement and darkness was interrupted when the key turned silently in the steel door, and the older woman stepped inside.

"Oh, how good of you to come again," exclaimed Meiling as her eyes adjusted with difficulty to the light. "Is this the beginning of my third day?" she asked.

"It is 7 A.M.," she replied. "I brought you a biscuit and another orange," she said as she patted Meiling's arm. "You are a very brave girl. God will reward you for your faithfulness. Someone will come for you later. I will be praying because they are shocked that you have not already succumbed to their wishes."

"I will never give in to them," Meiling answered emphatically. "Jesus means more to me than anything they can offer me, and if heaven is my next stop, I am ready."

"I must go. God be with you," the woman said as she slipped quietly out of the door.

Some hours later, the lights came on again, and a nurse stepped in and told Meiling she was to get ready to meet the supervisor once again. She brought her a basin of water and a towel to freshen herself for the interview.

A few minutes later, Meiling walked into the supervisor's office feeling a little shaky after lying on the hard boards in the dark for three days.

"So, you're here again," the supervisor said with a sneer on her face. "You didn't call to be released," she commented with raised eyebrows. "Most people respond quickly to this form of re-education, but you Christians are different. How can you resist like this?" Then, without waiting for an answer, she continued, "Oh, don't bother telling me. Your answers are all the same. You all say God was with you and helped you! What nonsense. I haven't seen God around here yet!"

She paused, and looking at Meiling, asked, "Well, what is your answer? Will you work for Mr. Ma or not?"

Meiling stood straight and tall, and looking the supervisor straight in the eye, she answered, "Nothing has changed. I will do anything Mr. Ma desires me to do that is legitimate work, but I will not be his mistress."

"You fool," she retorted with bitter venom in her voice. "But how can you look so calm and beautiful," she asked with a puzzled look. "Well, suit yourself, but I feel sorry for you," she said with a tinge of fear in her voice. "Follow me," she ordered.

"Here she is," she stated simply to Mr. Ma as the two entered the room. "I was unsuccessful in getting the commitment you wanted. I did my best as you directed. Please excuse me now. I have many things to do," she said as she quickly backed out of the door.

"So you still refuse my very generous offer," he asked with genuine surprise. "Do you understand that you are refusing 300 yuan a month? That is twice as much as the supervisor makes."

"My first allegiance is to Jesus Christ," Meiling replied quietly. "I cannot disobey His commands. I will serve you faithfully and well as a secretary or helper in anyway you wish. However, I cannot yield to your demands on matters of morality."

"How dare you lecture me," he screamed at the top of his voice. "I will teach you who is in charge here. What is right and wrong is determined by me, and me alone!" he thundered.

At that moment, Meiling felt strong and invincible as God's voice assured her He was with her. She intuitively knew she should not flinch or appear to be afraid. Mr. Ma strode toward her with uncontrollable anger shaking his whole body. Shouting to the supervisor to come, he pushed Meiling roughly toward her.

"Take her to the courtyard," he ordered. "Have all workers present to watch the discipline of this stupid girl."

A few minutes later as all the hospital workers assembled, they stood in mute silence wondering what was going to happen to Meiling.

"Take off her shirt," Ma bellowed, "and tie her hands to the post. I will teach her not to disobey my orders. I will turn her back into mincemeat. I guarantee she will never forget this lesson," he vowed as he continued shouting in anger.

The supervisor had witnessed many horrible things since the Communists took over the city, but she shuddered as she took off Meiling's shirt and tied her hands to the ring on the post. Once before she had witnessed Mr. Ma's anger as he had whipped an unfortunate man into unconsciousness. She actually felt sorry for Meiling. She whispered urgently in her ear, "It's not too late. Save yourself."

Meiling smiled shyly and whispered back, "I love Jesus too much to do that."

Ma picked up the bullwhip as he continued to shake with rage, and raised it above his head to send a searing blow to the bare back of this young girl who dared to cross him.

Just as he was about to strike the first blow, he screamed in agony. He gripped his heart and slumped to the ground, the whip falling harmlessly to the ground. Every head turned in his direction, not quite certain what was happening. Instead of seeing a young woman crying out in pain, there lay her tormentor, writhing on the ground in agony.

"Get a doctor," he gasped.

Moments later, he was wheeled into a hospital room as a doctor worked desperately to save his life. Meiling was forgotten, but all she could do was praise God for His unexpected intervention. After a few minutes the supervisor returned, and without a word, untied her hands and simply said, "Here's your shirt. Go home, and report for work in the morning."

As she was preparing to leave, several of the girls who worked with her, gathered around her and said, "You were so brave, Meiling! Do you believe your God saved you today?"

"Yes, I certainly do," she answered. "God spared me today. He is a wonderful God and a friend in time of trouble. But even if I had been whipped, my God would have given me the strength to endure."

During the next month, Meiling continued her regular work as before, only now every worker watched her with awe. *Is the Christian's God so powerful He can deliver someone from an angry administrator with the absolute power of life and death?* they whispered among themselves.

Ma made a slow recovery. He felt he had been humiliated before all the workers and he seethed inwardly. He vowed that as soon as he was well enough he would administer the punishment Meiling deserved. *I must punish her publicly or my authority will be undermined and I will lose face,* he reasoned. His doctor warned him that another fit of rage could be his last. He planned to have someone else administer the whipping; but he was determined to make a public spectacle so everyone would remember.

It was only a few days after he returned to his desk that he ordered Meiling tied to the post again. A very strong workman was ordered to administer twelve lashes of the whip on her bare back. As before, the stage was set. All the workers of the hospital were required to stand and observe the punishment. Before the beating took place, Ma strode up and down before the gathered workers, lecturing them about the policies of the Communist government and how they would be administered by him. He wanted to make it clear to everyone that severe punishment would be administered if anyone dared disobey his commands.

"Listen to me," he bellowed for all to hear. "Our government does not tolerate anyone's disobedience. This girl has refused to obey my orders, and in this hospital as in our government, that is inexcusable. Besides, the People's Republic of China does not believe that there is a God anywhere. Those who insist on spreading the ideas of the imperialists must be punished. Our New China has freed the people from all of these religious superstitions," he hissed as his blood pressure began to rise. "You are watching the punishment of this girl who is disloyal to our great leader and to me so that you will know you cannot do what she has done." His face contorted in anger. "Those who do will feel the full power of our great leader and government. No one can refuse to follow my orders and go unpunished. Do you all understand?" he screamed, staring at each one in turn. Finally, in the deathly silence of that moment, he turned to the strong workman designated to whip Meiling. "Get ready to administer the punishment," he ordered. "When I lower my arm, begin the lashes."

Tension filled the air as the crowd waited breathlessly. Every eye was on Mr. Ma whose face was livid with rage. He trembled as anger surged through his body. He was going to show his power and create fear in the workers. He raised his arm slowly as he relished this moment. The air fairly crackled with tension and dread. The longer he took, the better he liked it. *No one ever crosses Ma,* he gloated, *and gets away with it!* He looked around at the terrified workers—mostly young girls who shook with fright as they waited for the first searing lash. None of them wanted to be there, because they feared it could be them being humiliated just as easily as Meiling, *but why was she so stubborn?* they thought. *Why not give in? Why not accept the excellent pay and save your life? But then, Meiling was so different from all of them. She really believed that her God was going to save her in some mysterious way!* And they had seen it a few weeks earlier, but what would happen now?

Gloating over this moment of triumph, Ma looked around and enjoyed the terror in the eyes of the workers. *I have them right where I want them,* he thought. *From now on they will all do my bidding.* He stretched his arm a little higher as if to emphasize his point. The man with the whip watched intently, knowing that if he failed to fulfill his part in this awful travesty, he could be the next one tied to the post. The whip was poised; ready to be unleashed the moment Ma's arm came down. He watched and waited as the tension grew.

Then, suddenly Ma was groveling on the ground again, crying out in agony. In an instant, his gloating had turned against him. He gasped, clutched his chest and cried out in pain. The man lowered the whip.

"Help me," Ma pleaded hoarsely as a doctor bent over him.

The supervisor rushed over to Meiling, quickly untied her wrists. "Leave immediately, and don't come back for a week," she warned with a puzzled look on her face.

Thirty minutes later, Ma was pronounced dead. The news spread like wildfire throughout the hospital to workers and patients alike. Awe settled on the hospital staff as they remembered Meiling's words that she expected her God to save her. "Who is this God anyway?" they asked one another fearfully.

A smile spread across Meiling's face as she hurriedly left the building and headed home. God had spoken loudly. The supervisor and all the staff had gotten the message.

"Thank You, Jesus. You won another victory and Your name will be glorified."

Since the sudden death of the hospital administrator, conditions at the hospital deteriorated for Meiling. Fearful that her position might be at stake, Meiling's supervisor began to make many unreasonable demands. Frightened supervisors and workers were afraid that somehow they would be implicated in Mr. Ma's death. There was nothing else to do than take out their fear and frustrations on Meiling. Life became one nightmare after another, but through it all, she stood the test. When asked how she could stand it, she simply responded that Jesus living in her made her strong. Amazed, they stood in awe of this beautiful girl who would not bend.

Forced relocation of city young people to remote farming areas of the country as a means of re-education was underway. Mao had decreed that re-education through hard labor on a farm would set them free from the old capitalist views and bring them under his control. The Great Leap Forward program was launched to the detriment of the country.

The new hospital administrator discussed the problem of Meiling with his staff. It was decided that they should waste no time in recommending her deportation to a distant farm—the farther away the better!

"Under the circumstances, this is the safest thing we can do for the hospital," the administrator said one day as he met with his staff. "We cannot afford to jeopardize the reputation of the hospital by retaining her services, and besides, because of her insubordination, she was responsible for Mr. Ma's death," he added, choosing his words with care as he tried to dignify his decision.

There were no dissenting voices. Instead, all concurred that it would impress the director of hospitals and be recorded that they were vigilant in weeding out unreliable workers for the re-education program. Two weeks later, the administrator received a glowing letter of commendation for his outstanding vigilance and recommendation. At the weekly political rally, he read the order: "By order of the Hubei provincial government, Woo Meiling is ordered relocated immediately to a work camp at a communal farm in north China."

A placard was hung around Meiling's neck with the words 'un-reliable worker' written in large characters. The administrator then read off the trumped up charges.

"Woo Meiling," intoned the administrator, "has been found guilty not only of the serious charge of insubordination, but also of propagating the superstitious ideas of religion, and particularly Christianity, which is forbidden in our New China."

Her friends sat in stunned silence with downcast eyes as the administrator continued the reading of the long list of lies he called serious charges. Her friends knew they were all false. They had watched as she courageously resisted the advances and demands of Mr. Ma. And then, to add insult to injury, following the reading of the charges, they were all instructed to vote their approval of the punishment by raising their right hand. Fighting hard to control their true feelings, they all reluctantly raised their hands as the leader carefully scrutinized the crowd. With their eyes firmly fixed on the floor before them, they dared not look at Meiling as she was marched out like a common criminal. All felt the sting of the betrayal of their good friend, but feared that they would be next if they resisted. Again, the government had triumphed using fear as the main instrument for keeping the masses under control.

The next morning, a heartbroken Mrs. Woo arrived at the detention center with Meiling's bedding roll, a few items of clothing and other small necessities, neatly tied up in a bundle. She was allowed five minutes to bid her daughter farewell.

"Oh, my poor child," she wept. "What have they done to you? They've taken my husband, my home, and now my precious child. Oh, God," she cried, "I can't take any more."

Meiling held her mother in a close embrace as she comforted her. "Mother, do not despair. God is always in control. He is sending me on a mission. There are people who need to know Him, and He has chosen us to be part of His plan to reach them. I will miss you so much, but I will pray for you every day, and for Father, too. Some day we will be reunited."

"You are so young, so beautiful," she said as she clung to her daughter. "You are the pride of China, not a criminal! I am so proud of you and your testimony for God. Yes, our God is faithful in the worst of times just as He is in the best. Write to me as soon as you can with an address."

"All right, time's up," a gruff voice announced.

The two women clung to each other a few more seconds, only releasing each other at a second harsh command.

"God bless you till we meet again," they whispered as they parted.

Meiling was ushered out of the room by the guards as Mrs. Woo watched in despair, with tears streaming down her face.

A woman attendant touched her arm as she gently said, "I'm sorry. Now you must go."

Mrs. Woo turned to leave, and looking at the woman who spoke tenderly to her, she replied, "My only hope is in Jesus who never leaves us nor forsakes us."

"But not many people have such hope these days," replied the guard. Then, realizing what a dangerous statement she had made, she gently guided Mrs. Woo to the front door, and without another word, closed it after her.

Life in the commune was anything but easy. Planting rice all day long was a backbreaking job for the girls from the city who were unaccustomed to such hard physical labor. For long hours they moved through the stinking mud, planting rice plants by hand, row upon row, as their ancestors had done for centuries. Weary and aching in every joint, they returned at night to crude bathhouses where they cleansed themselves as best they could with little water and no soap. Some wept bitterly over their plight, while others shouted obscenities at the authorities; that is, all but Meiling. She endured the pain quietly and sought to ease the suffering of the others.

"Where do you get the fortitude to act like this?" a young woman asked one night as they bathed.

"I have an inner peace that helps me endure the pain and suffering," she said simply, since it was too dangerous to talk openly. People sought to gain even small privileges from their taskmasters when they reported gossip, some true and most untrue. It didn't really matter as long as the supervisor considered them good Communists reporting on others.

"But where does it come from?" she persisted. "Under these circumstances, it must be supernatural!"

"What do you mean?" Meiling asked guardedly.

"Just that," the girl replied. "I have a grandmother who acts and talks like you, and she is a Christian." Pausing a moment, she asked pointedly, "Are you one?"

Looking the girl squarely in the eye, she searched to see if there was sincerity in her question.

"Believe me," she responded as Meiling looked deeply into her eyes, "I am not one of them, but I am hurting and lonely. There is something about you that reminds me of my grandmother."

Relieved, Meiling responded, "I believe you. This is a difficult place to be, and except for my faith in Jesus Christ, I would be as frustrated as you," she admitted. "He is my daily hope, and a friend who is better than the closest relative," she spoke softly, looking around carefully to be sure no one was eavesdropping. "It is not safe to talk openly with anyone like this," she continued, "but I believe you are sincere. I would be glad to help you find Him as your Savior."

"Oh, would you?" the girl responded hopefully. "Please tell me everything you can so I will have the same peace and help."

Over the next months, this friendship grew as did the girl's faith. Without any opportunity to meet with other believers, and without any Scriptures except the words Meiling had memorized before being sent to the commune, they both grew in the Lord. They had to be extremely careful with whom they talked about their faith lest they be betrayed to the authorities. One thing they could not hide was the radiance of their faces. That spoke volumes, and gradually, one by one, others sought to know this Jesus they saw in the two girls.

After almost a year in the commune, Meiling anxiously looked forward to the annual letter she was permitted to receive from her family. Her mother wrote that in spite of her father's suffering in the mine, his faith had grown strong through his contacts with the elderly Pastor Wong who was also a prisoner there. Anching's father had been demoted for his faith, nothing had been heard of Anching, their church was closed, and Pastor Yang had been sent to a stone quarry for twenty years of indoctrination!

Yes, Meiling thought as she read the letter through blinding tears that flowed unchecked down her cheeks, *the river has run red with pain and suffering for my family and many believers.* Blinded by the scalding tears, she clasped her letter to her breast and cried out to God for His help in this awful hour of need. Then through her tears there burst forth a song in her heart. *The flood and the fire had not overcome them just as the Word promised.*

Oh, how she longed for the day when once again she could raise her voice and sing aloud the glorious praises of God. *Our church is closed, but Jesus, You're still very much alive in China! My father is down in the blackness of a coalmine, but thank God, You are there with him. Anching is somewhere I am sure, and You are watching over him. Oh, thank You Jesus, even in the midst of the flood and the heat of this fire, no one will be able to overcome us! Thank You, Jesus, Your Word says that if You are for us, who can be against us? That's Your promise, and I stand upon it.*

She brushed the tears from her eyes as a joyous thought flooded her heart. *There is another river! The river of the precious blood of Jesus that flowed from Calvary and touched my life, my family, and Anching and his family. It cleansed us all, and it is cleansing our land even though at this moment we cannot see it all.*

Whenever they had opportunity, the few believers spoke softly with each other in secluded spots, even for a few minutes, and they lifted up their voices in praise to God. He was right there with them in the midst of the flood. He had not forsaken them though the fires burned ever so hot. There was hope that one day the night would be over and China would burst forth like a beautiful flower and the whole world would know that Jesus still reigns. He is in control of all things.

This is not what I would have chosen for my life, Meiling thought. *No, by this time, Anching and I should have been nearing graduation from Wuhan University and looking forward to life together serving God. Instead, here I am a prisoner in this miserable com-*

mune, *Father is suffering in the coalmines, and my poor mother! Oh God, how she is suffering! And where is Anching? Is he still alive? Will we ever meet again?*

Meditating on the Word as she stuck one rice plant in the mud after another, she was reminded that this light affliction is but for a season. The Holy Spirit brought to her memory the words of Peter, "But how is it to your credit if you receive a beating for your wrong doing and endure it? But if you suffer for doing good and you endure it, this is commendable before God. To this you were called, because Christ suffered for you, leaving you an example, that you should follow in His steps" (1 Peter 2:20–21).

Lord, she prayed, help me to be faithful day after day, and to trust You with my circumstances. By faith I believe the day will come when this awful night will be past, and my family will be reunited once again. And, Lord, somehow I believe I'll meet Anching again.

She paused in her planting for a few moments, and looking up at the clouds in the azure blue sky, she smiled, and breathed a prayer: *Yes, Lord, I will trust You to work all things out.*

EPILOGUE

The heroism and fortitude of the Chinese believers, who passed through the terrible decades of the 50s and 60s when the Communists were solidifying their stranglehold on the people of China, will be continued in the next volume, Exiles of Hope. These decades were filled with violence and the unbelievable persecution of the church, and the characters of volume one.

Anching and Meiling and their friend Wenpei are typical of millions of believers in China and around the world who suffer horrible crimes at the hands of evil people. Nevertheless, they endure, having seen the Lord, and gladly lay down their lives for Him.

Today in China, reform has gripped the national leadership, but still there is that deep-seated fear of Christianity. The suffering continues for many; thousands still languish in slave labor camps making cheap products for world consumption. Pastors and leaders are still arrested, beaten, deprived of liberty and sometimes life itself. Yet, in the midst of the fear and hostility, there is a movement of God in progress that gives one the impression that whole new chapters of the book of Acts are being written today. Many have said that what is happening in China is the most amazing movement of God in the history of the country.

Exiles of Hope is the continuing saga of Anching and Meiling, who against all odds believed God and refused to give up their faith in Jesus Christ, even though it entailed suffering and long years of privation. Volume two continues this story of their search for each other. It is an amazing story of faith and courage that will help us all focus our eyes on Jesus for the hour of suffering we also may face in the near future.

You may follow the progress of volume two in the months ahead on the author's web site or by contacting him at his e-mail address.

Web Site: *http://www.bollback.com*
E-mail: *Kahu@juno.com*

To order additional copies of

RED RUNS
THE
RIVER

Have your credit card ready and call:
1-877-421-READ (7323)
or please visit our web site at

www.pleasantword.com
Also available at: www.amazon.com

Printed in the United States
22613LVS00004B/64-81